NIGHT STALKER

A TOME OF BILL ADVENTURE

RICK GUALTIERI

Edited by Curiosity Quills Press:
https://curiosityquills.com/

Cover by Mallory Rock at
www.rocksolidbookdesign.com

Published by Freewill Press
Freewill-press.com

DEDICATION

For all of those who dream of one day donning a mask, a cape, and a pair of tights. May the forces of evil quake in your presence.

Author's Note: This story is set roughly halfway between the events of *Bill The Vampire* and *Scary Dead Things*. It contains spoilers for *Bill The Vampire*.

JUST ANOTHER DAY AMONG THE DEAD

"We are the masters of the night, the lords of darkness. Who are you to dare tell us that this city is off limits to our appetites?"

I blinked a few times, trying to process the bullshit I was hearing. "Did you steal that from a movie or something?"

"What?" the long-haired asshole in front of me asked.

I kept forgetting what his real name was – the guy just wasn't worth the cycles required of my frontal lobe – but he went by the ridiculous moniker of Dusk Reaper. Yeah, I know, pretty fucking stupid, but up until a few months ago that was the norm for the coven of vampires I was in charge of. "You heard me. How the fuck can you even say something like that with a straight face?"

Dusk Reaper glared at me, his fangs protruding ever so slightly from his upper lip. Oh the drama.

You'd have thought I'd asked him to pull down his pants and bend over while I retrieved an extra-long mop handle. The reality was, I'd walked in, hoping for a quiet evening of relaxing and maybe ogling the voluptuous females who made up roughly half the coven. Instead, I'd found this fucker along with a dead body he was tearing into like a hyena.

Ignoring that I'd been trying to rein in the coven's habit of – well, there was no real way to explain it otherwise – being mass murderers when the mood suited them, this dickhead was taking it a step further by making a mess of things. Jeez! You'd have thought he was a toddler with a big slice of birthday cake. It was sure as shit gonna take a bit more than a few wet wipes to clean this up.

The situation was made worse because he wasn't alone. Eliza, a cute brunette vamp, lay on the couch in just her bra and panties, copious amounts of blood dripping from her exposed flesh. It was obvious I'd interrupted them, cock-blocking before they could engage in what would have probably been some truly disturbing sex.

That last part really ticked me off. I normally couldn't care less about fetishes, but fuck that shit. I was the goddamned coven master here. All the glory was supposed to be mine, not to mention all the poon ... in theory anyway.

During my first few weeks as leader, it had seemed that would be the case. However, at some point, I'd apparently made a wrong turn and somehow ended up in, well, maybe not the friend zone, but definitely the no fucking zone. And here was Dusk Reaper – a known asshole – about to score with one of the many hotties of Village Coven, *my* coven. Talk about life, or the afterlife, being unfair.

"Listen," I said, trying to talk sense into this senseless fucktard, "I know you guys have to eat. Believe me, I'm not trying to starve anyone. But this…" I waved my arms to indicate the scene before me. "This is going a little overboard, especially since the larder is full of bagged blood."

We were in what was known throughout the coven as the Loft. It occupied the entire third floor of this building and served as a sort of vamp frat house. It also had a special place in my heart being the very spot I had died roughly three months earlier. Okay fine, maybe *special* wasn't quite the best word to describe it. Still, if there's one place that came to mind when I thought about vampires, this was it.

And what a place, possessing all the comforts of *home*: blacked out windows, reinforced doors, stain resistant carpet, and access to pretty much every cable channel known to man. Below us was empty space, sound-proofing against any screams that might be overheard – something I was also trying to curb. On the ground floor lay a fairly busy techno club, which the coven occasionally used as a convenient hunting ground. When that wasn't feasible, though, one needed only to walk down another flight of steps to the basement level. That's the larder I mentioned, a storage room connected to the sewers, housing several industrial sized refrigerators that I knew damn well were fully stocked.

Dusk Reaper took a step forward, oddly bold this

evening. Maybe he didn't want to look like a pussy in front of his piece du jour. "You would ask that we sate our hunger with mere bagged blood? Do you think us cattle? We are predators, lions stalking the desert."

"The Savannah," I corrected – dumbass. When he just stood there, staring blankly at me, I continued. "I don't care if you think you're a lion, a furry, or My Little fucking Pony, I don't want..."

"Have you ever made love in the still steaming blood of a human?" Eliza interrupted, ruining any focus I might've had that evening. My earlier plan of popping in to see what was playing on HBO might as well have happened in a whole other lifetime. I glanced away from Dick Raper and toward her, most certainly noticing her idly fingering the flimsy lace that made up her bra.

"Um ... can't say that I have," I replied like some sort of idiot. Goddamn it! If I had one weakness – aside from looking like a dumpy nerd, being a relatively young and weak vampire, and having no real fucking clue as to what I was doing – it was women. To say that my dating life was a wee bit barren as of late was an understatement.

"Maybe if you tried, you'd rethink your stance." Her voice was innocence itself, but it carried an undertone that would have made an experienced whore shiver. Within seconds, my pants began to feel two sizes too small.

Although I doubt he had any intention of helping me, Dusk Reaper's petty nature saved me from going full retard as I struggled to come up with an answer to her very logical sounding statement. His eyes flashed black and he snarled. "Do not get any ideas, *Freewill.*"

He spat that last part as if it were meant to be an insult, but I'd been throwing one-liners with my friends ever since my playground days. I could come up with a better zinger in my sleep. Besides, he was right. I *was* what they called a Freewill – a vampire variant of a sort; the name implying an ability to resist the compulsions of older vampires. It was an ability I was damned glad to have. Stupid name aside, it was a handy power to have in a hierarchy of beings that were used to lording their might over those weaker than them.

In some ways it was nice to be special. A smile crossed my lips at the thought. Unfortunately, the douche-canoe in front of me apparently took it as a signal to continue. "She is mine to use as I see fit this night."

I locked eyes with him, Eliza's spell broken, and put a little iron into my tone. "First off, my name is Bill. Second, you two can do whatever the fuck you want, but not this way. Bottom line is I don't want to see shit like this again. It's just ... sick."

With that, I turned away, my plans for the evening thwarted. Even if I'd told those two to scram, it's not like I'd be too keen to sit on the couch and channel surf while congealed blood oozed through the seat of my pants. Goddamn it. Vampires could be so fucking gross when they wanted to be.

I headed downstairs and contemplated the bar on the ground floor for a moment before moving on. All things considered, it was probably not the best place to show my face. The clientele there was young, even younger than my twenty-four years – this being a tragically hip SoHo joint. Being the sort who enjoyed a weekend of gaming around the D&D table, I'd stand out like a sore thumb.

That in of itself didn't bother me much, but I also happened to be in charge of the monsters who occasionally prowled down there. All it would take would be one person with a few more brain cells than average to put two and two together and I'd probably end up at One Police Plaza trying to explain that I wasn't an accomplice to mass murder.

Okay, maybe that's less likely than I was letting on. I'd been told that the vampire nation kept the higher-ups of this city well-greased for such *situations*. Still, why bother taking unnecessary chances?

Speaking of the one who'd done that telling, though, I decided that rather than head back home, maybe I'd make one other stop while in coven territory. At the very least, Sally was pleasant to look at, if a total bitch to listen to.

2

WHERE THE WORK NEVER ENDS

The Office, as it was unofficially called, was rapidly becoming the center of coven activity in this city. Back during the reign of Night Razor, the previous master, it had been primarily used as storage as well as a nest during daylight hours. Considering its proximity to NYU, this made it a handy spot for vampires to crash after a night of hunting coeds.

Under my rule, though...

Oh who was I kidding? I ran Village Coven on paper, sure, but in reality I was a figurehead at best. The real power behind the throne lay with Sally, my so-called silent partner. The problem there was twofold: she wasn't particularly silent and, as far as our partnership was concerned, she considered herself first among not-so-equals.

She was a fifty-year old vamp in the body of a twenty-something stripper – and what a body it was. She had a figure to die for – quite literally.

That in of itself made her dangerous, but what made her truly lethal was her mind. Though she looked as hot, or better, than any of the other glamourous Village Coven babes, she was far from being the vapid fashion model the majority of them aspired toward. She possessed a quick wit, a venomous tongue, and a complete disregard for anything that stood in her way – including pesky things like the law.

I reminded myself of these things as I rode the elevator up to our main floor. I stepped out and found myself in a dank expanse of a room. The smell was overpowering, even to me. Bodies hung from meat hooks and rats scurried to lap up any of a dozen pools of blood that lay in this accursed place.

Just kidding!

Shit like that only exists in the movies. In the real world such things tend to not go unnoticed for long, especially in a city this size. Also, the smarter vamps were just as grossed out by crap like that as any sane person.

Though I seemed to always just miss getting a peek at our bank books, I was well aware that the coven was flush was cash. One didn't own several pieces of prime Manhattan real estate only to spend their nights eating out of dumpsters – well, unless one were batshit crazy.

Sally wasn't, though. The pristine carpet on the floor, expensive looking paintings lining the wall, and hardwood double doors at the end of the hall all attested to a sense of power and wealth. Hell, this place made the online gaming company where I was still forced to earn a paycheck look like a shithole in comparison. Still, all of this was fairly new too. Sally had wasted little time in switching the coven's focus from the SoHo loft to this place.

I approached the door and tried the handle – locked. Okay, that wasn't too surprising. I mean, it was well after dark and our floors were surrounded by actual legit businesses that kept relatively normal hours. If we left things opened up at all hours of the night, we'd either look like what we were – a coven of bloodthirsty beasts – or an escort service.

Unfortunately, despite being lord and master of this merry bunch of monsters, I somehow didn't have a key – forcing me to knock like I was here to deliver a late night pizza. My enhanced strength helped ensure that even the thickest doors didn't fully muffle my entreaties for entrance. Regardless, I still had to wait several seconds before my acute undead hearing picked up the sound of footsteps approaching.

The door cracked open and a pretty brown face surrounded by a permed cascade of black hair greeted me. Alice. She was a rarity among vamps – a sweetheart who actually cared. I didn't really consider that a recipe for longevity amidst a group of psycho assholes, but to each their own.

Anyway, she'd been somewhat jittery around me the first few weeks I'd been in charge. Sally and I had been forced to put a bit of a scare in her and the others during my first month as a vampire. It had been a case of either earn their respect or end up permanently dead. All of our machinations had been bullshit, of course, and, judging by the unflinching way she stared at me from the half-open door, I suspected she was beginning to understand that.

"Oh, hi, Bill." She sounded disappointed as if she'd been expecting someone else. Not quite the welcome wagon one would expect for the head honcho. Oh well, it was still better than the greeting I'd gotten from Dusk Reaper.

Not being the type to complain about a nonviolent hello from a beautiful woman, I gave her my best 'please give me a pity fuck' smile and then stepped in.

The place was a mess of construction, with various coven members scurrying back and forth on some errand or other. Sally was having the place gutted, but for reasons she didn't elaborate on other than to tell me it was time to inject this coven with a modicum of professionalism. Considering the dress that Alice was wearing, as well as the attire of some of the other ladies present, a part of me wondered if I was standing in the beginning act of *Bordello of Blood*. Oddly enough, I wasn't entirely against that concept. Go figure.

I opened my mouth to ask where Sally was, when her voice rang out from somewhere further in. "Who's at the door, Star? That had better not be fucking Brian back so soon. There's no way that asshole could score some..." She stepped around a corner near the back and stopped when she saw me. "Oh ... it's you."

It wasn't her words that struck me as strange so

much as her tone. Normally, Sally was a hundred pounds of attitude in a size four dress. Her clothes were often sharp, but not nearly as much as her fangs or tongue. Tonight, though, she appeared to falter when she walked into the room. Despite knowing that she had no pulse to speak of, I could have sworn her face turned a shade paler at the sight of me.

"Freewill," she said with a reverent nod of her head.

I couldn't help but notice all activity in the room had ceased as vamps turned to watch us. Okie-doke then. What a bunch of fucking weirdos.

"What?" I asked, after a moment of uncomfortable silence. "You expecting the FedEx guy or something?"

Several eyes hardened in my direction and I saw a few sets of fangs being flashed my way. Jeez, you tell one bad joke...

"Starlight," Sally said, addressing Alice by her former coven name – the one she'd discarded when Night Razor's rule had ended, "I need to talk to our esteemed master. Please wrap up here and then dismiss the team for the evening."

Again her tone was strange – no hint of attitude, just pure seriousness. Hell, I almost didn't recognize her. It wasn't exactly like her to not at least throw a sarcastic eye-roll my way.

Alice nodded at Sally's request, although she didn't need to do much to let the rest of the place know. Vampires have ridiculously good hearing, so it was a safe bet that every set of ears on the floor had heard them being given the night off. A few moments later, this was confirmed as more coven members – many looking like they'd just stepped out of an Abercrombie and Fitch catalog – came into view. Most of them barely paid me any heed as they headed to the door, although I could have sworn I caught at least some shade from the various gazes that did meet mine. What the fuck?

I walked toward Sally as the rank and file continued their escape, no doubt wanting to get the fuck out of Dodge lest she change her mind and put their asses back to work.

As I approached to within ten feet, she trembled and took what appeared to be an involuntary step back. Sally was a petite thing, barely five feet in heels, but she seemed to shrink in on herself becoming even smaller, more vulnerable looking.

"Is all to your liking, coven master?" she asked timidly.

"Sure. Just peachy." I couldn't help but be worried. What the hell had spooked her so badly? Had someone in the coven rebelled and challenged her ... my ... err ... *our* authority? Had we been attacked? I knew there was another nearby nest of vampires, the Howard Beach Coven – HBC for short. They had a mad-on for me thanks to a misunderstanding from a few months back. Had that finally escalated into something worse?

The sound of the front door slamming shut came from behind me, echoing in the now mostly empty space. I glanced back at Sally and saw her spying the door over my shoulder, her head cocked as if listening for something.

After a few seconds of uncomfortable silence, I opened my mouth to question her odd behavior, but a fist to my face derailed that train of thought before it could leave the station.

3

WHEN IN ROME

The funny thing about vampires is that they completely upend how we normally perceive both power and threat. It's not size that matters in the world of the undead, but age. Through methods I didn't quite understand, a vampire's strength seemed to be directly related to their time spent upon this Earth. One would normally take a look at someone like Sally and assume that a strong gust of wind could knock her over. That was a mistake. Though young by vamp standards, she had enough years behind her that she could have pimp-slapped me if we came to blows.

Case in point how I found myself on the floor, staring at the ceiling, and waiting for my accelerated healing to kick in and reset my jaw. I'd been hit harder during my short tenure as a vamp, but that didn't make her punch any less unpleasant. Oh well, at least I hadn't been knocked the fuck out.

I opened my mouth to speak, but first had to

swallow a mouthful of blood, having nearly bitten my tongue in two when she'd connected. She used the delay to spin on her heel toward the rear of the floor.

"Get your fat ass up and into my office ... *now*."

Gone was the timid flower of just a few moments earlier and in her place stood the Sally I'd come to know and ... well, let's just say love wasn't the first word that sprung to mind.

Wait ... *her office?*

Curious, I picked myself off the floor and followed as bidden.

She wasn't kidding. Though most of the place was in disarray, the corner office – featuring a view that the executives at my company would have gladly killed each other for – was much further along. She took a seat in a leather executive chair behind a solid looking mahogany desk. Hell, she even had one of those Newton's cradle toys to round out things.

I stepped inside and she nodded toward a chair in front of her desk. Feeling like I was about to be dressed down for some stupid corporate slight, I sat and waited to see what she had to say. I didn't have to wait long.

"What the fuck are you doing?" she snarled, all trace of vulnerability gone.

"Is there a gas leak or something here?" I asked. "Because you're acting a bit strange if I might say so."

She raised an eyebrow and I could see a vein pop in her forehead ... quite the feat for someone with no heartbeat. "Do you think this is a joke?"

I reached over and lifted one of the balls of her desk toy. I let go and enjoyed the clack-clack sound they made as they bounced off each other. "Well, I guess this whole being dead thing is sort of a..."

Quick as a snake, she grabbed hold of the cradle and crushed it in her hand. The steel balls, loose of their moorings, rolled across the desk and clattered to the floor – loud in the silence of the room. "In about two seconds those are gonna be yours."

"So you're going to touch my balls?"

Sally's eyes flashed black at my snark, and for a second there I was certain she'd launch herself across the desk and throttle me. Needless to say, she was unusually testy tonight.

Fortunately for me, she took a deep breath and sat back in her chair – a chair much more comfortable looking than the ass-cracker my butt was in. After a moment, she looked me in the eye, pity now coloring her expression, and asked, "You have no fucking clue what's going on, do you?"

"I just got here," I replied with a shrug. "All I saw was Alice giving me some attitude, followed by you acting like an extra from *Texas Chainsaw Massacre*. Speaking of which, did I hear you call her Starlight?"

"Yeah," she replied with a dismissive wave.

"Why?"

"It's the same thing as Dusk Reaper. She decided she preferred her old coven name. A lot of the members are reverting back."

"So they'd rather have stupid X-men code names?"

"I don't know, maybe it makes them feel special or something."

"Is that a fact ... *Sally Sunset*?"

She leaned forward and glared. "Say that stupid last name Night Razor saddled me with again and I'll show you just how *special* I can be, *Dr. Death*."

"Relax." I held up my hands in mock surrender, inwardly sighing at the mention of my own idiotic coven name – sadly of my own choosing. "No need for violence."

She rolled her eyes at me. "That's the problem. You're headed down the road toward a lot of violence, more than you bargained for in fact."

"Just for the record, I didn't really bargain for any."

She ignored me and went on. "Did you see them all out there?"

"Uh ... yeah."

"It wasn't just Star."

I thought back to a few short minutes earlier. Come to think of it, there had been an overabundance of hostility in the air. I'd dismissed it, though. I mean, they're vampires for Christ's sake. When were they not contemplating violence? Even so, during my short tenure among the undead I'd learned a few things – first and foremost being that there was a strict hierarchy of command. Vampires might act all badass around humans, but the second a higher ranking vamp walked into the room they'd turn into a can of instant pussy – just add water.

That had been the case with me, at least before tonight. As far as they were all aware, I'd taken the mantle of leadership from their former top dog. That made me the head honcho. As a result, my initial days as coven master had been filled with all sorts of ass-kissing and compliments toward my power. As someone who'd been force fed his fair share of slices from the bully cake in high school, I was well aware of how a little power could corrupt. Be that as it may, it was still fucking awesome! I could understand what absolute dictators saw in the job.

I thought about this for a few moments before asking, "All of that shit was directed at me?"

"Why the fuck did you think I put on that act out there? It certainly wasn't because I was in awe of your mad leadership skills."

"What? I thought my tough guy act was pretty convincing."

"For a first grade play perhaps." She stood up and turned toward one of the plate glass windows, staring out at the nighttime cityscape. "Face it. You've been slipping."

"I have?"

She glanced backed toward me, a frown creasing her mouth as if she found what she was about to say next distasteful. "How many of the coven have you slept with?"

"What?"

"You heard me. Who in the coven have you fucked since you've been in charge?"

"Um?"

"Elena? Patrice? Firebird? Any of them?"

"Well, no."

She shook her head in disgust. "At least you won't need a shot of penicillin from being with that last bitch."

"Huh?"

"Never mind. Do you see the problem here?"

"Not really."

"You do understand that Jeff had each and every one of them, right?" she asked, using Night Razor's rather mundane real name.

"You too, if I recall."

"Yes," she replied with gritted teeth. "*Me too.*"

I hadn't been around to personally experience it, but I'd heard enough to conclude that Jeff had treated the ladies of his coven like his own personal harem. From the sound of things, he'd also been happy to let any of the guys he favored partake in his sloppy seconds.

When I'd first taken over, I'd been nearly bowled over by all the flirtation going on. Women whom I'd normally never have a shot with, outside of maybe my porn fantasies, were throwing themselves at me – mine for the taking. The problem was, I'd been well aware of Jeff's douchebaggery. I wanted to create a different vibe with my rule, one based off of vampires behaving more human and less like filthy beasts of the night. As a result, tempting as it was – and oh God it was tempting – I'd decided to hold off for a while until such time as I'd earned a little bit of the coven's trust. At that point, I figured it would be a pussy feast that they'd sing about all the way in Valhalla.

Except that hadn't happened. Hell, after a while the flirting had dropped off to nothing and I'd found myself back to where I'd been as a human: staring at the eye candy, but unable to sate my sweet tooth.

I didn't like were this was going. "Okay, so I'm not a serial rapist. So what?"

"Exactly," she replied as if that told me anything. "So how about killing? Have you offed anyone in the coven yet?"

"Hell no!"

"What about a good old-fashioned ass-beating?" I opened my mouth to reply in the negative, but she held up a hand. "I already know the answer, genius. You may treat this coven as your weekend getaway from your two live-in boyfriends"—referring to my roommates Tom and Ed—"but I'm here twenty-four seven and, believe me, I keep an eye on these things."

"So let me get this straight. You're saying all that shit from earlier is because I've been a nice guy?"

"Yes," she replied, leaning over her desk and affording me a glimpse of her generous cleavage. She quickly snapped her fingers, directing my eyes back up to hers. "And you'd better believe that saying about nice guys is true, because your ass is about to come in dead last."

4

HOME AGAIN, HOME AGAIN

"Seriously? They want to kill me just because I'm being a decent person?"

"No." She stepped around her desk, sat upon it, and crossed one shapely leg over the other. It wasn't much, but in that one movement she made Eliza's nearly naked body look like a frump in comparison. "Being a decent person is just ticking them off."

"So then..."

"Losing their respect and coming across as a weak pansy-ass is what's making them want to kill you."

"How? As far as they know, I wiped the fucking floor with Jeff. Hell, then there's all that Freewill bull-shit you've been spreading."

Freewills were supposedly legendary warriors of the vampire race, but before I showed up it had been more than half a millennia since one had been *born*. As a result, the vast majority of the vamps I'd met knew little to nothing about them – most of the

RICK GUALTIERI

coven being far under a century in age. To them, Freewills were legend and myth with no basis in reality. Sally had used that to her advantage. Working with James, the vampire we reported to in the grand scheme of things, she'd spread enough rumors to ensure that most of the coven gave me a wide berth during those first few nights of my existence. She'd spread bullshit like a master chef making a plate of gold-covered truffles and it had worked.

"I'm well aware." She shook her head. "But then you had to go and fuck it up tonight."

"Wait. I haven't done anything tonight. I stopped by the Loft for a few minutes and then came here."

"And who was there?"

"Eliza and Dipshit Reaper."

"They weren't the only ones. Dread Stalker was in the other room with Vanessa."

Of course. Why wouldn't he be? Jeez, was I the only guy in this place who wasn't getting any? "Okay, so?"

"*So*, you pussed out in front of Dusk Reaper."

"I didn't puss out. I was gonna hang there, but then I saw that he was making a fucking mess. So I left."

"Oh? He didn't get in your face about anything?"

"Well, yeah a bit..."

"He didn't openly defy you?"

"Okay, he might have done that a little."

"And did you kick the ever-unliving shit out of him for it?"

"Not exactly."

"Not exactly?"

"I told him to clean up his mess and then I walked out."

"Yeah, well guess what, mighty Freewill, that's what's known as pussing out in the vampire world. You do not let an inferior give you lip and get away with it *ever*."

"I told him not to do it again."

"Did your parents ever tell you that when you were a kid?"

"All the time."

"Did it work?"

Hmm, she may have had a point there.

Sally stared me in the eye, her gaze softening ever so slightly as if she felt some pity for my situation. Unfortunately, her tongue didn't get the memo. "Here's the deal: Jeff could get away with telling us to never do something again because he was always making an example of someone. It didn't matter who. We *all* got a taste of it. Bottom line was we were all..." She hesitated for a moment.

"Afraid of him?"

Her eyes narrowed at me and I realized maybe that hadn't been the ideal choice of words. "I was going to say wary of getting on his bad side. During his reign, he didn't have any issues with using the tools given to him – fists or compulsion."

At least she didn't say brains, because from what I'd known of the guy he hadn't exactly been packing a lot in the intellect department. Even so, when you're the six-hundred pound gorilla in the room you don't really need to be a Rhodes Scholar.

I let our discussion sink in for a few moments.

Crap! And here I thought that the bullshit was behind me. I now saw that I'd merely crested a rise and found a whole new valley of it to traipse through.

At last I swallowed my pride, knowing Sally would probably skin me alive for it. "How badly did I fuck up?"

"Star is a good person to use for judging these things."

"She was definitely giving me the stink-eye tonight."

"Exactly," she replied, deadpan. "She's the type who wears her emotions on her sleeve. You'll notice she's been tiptoeing around you the past few months."

"Not tonight. I saw nothing but contempt on her face."

"Probably an act. Don't tell her I said this or I'll rip your nuts off, but she actually likes you."

I perked up a bit. "Oh?"

"Not like that, Romeo. You and she are a lot alike ... outside of the minor difference that she's gorgeous and you're you."

"Thanks for the ego boost."

She ignored me and continued. "You're both ... well, more or less human. She's not an abusive asshole like most of the membership. After Jeff, you're practically a ray of sunshine for someone like her. When the rumors started flying, though, I have little doubt she realized she had to make a choice. Unfortunately, for you ... and that means us ... she's just smart enough to know which way the odds are leaning."

"Rumors? Wait, what did Reaper do, start texting everyone the second I left?"

"More or less."

What an asshole! See, that's one of the things about the vampire lifestyle that drives me batshit. You'd think they'd all be a bunch of technology shunning monsters, content on skulking in dank tunnels until sunset hit and they swooped forth to prey upon the living. The reality was, in many ways modern covens more closely resembled high school cliques than anything. "So what now?"

"Now I try my best to do damage control. If they think you're weak, then they're gonna think your second-in-command is weak too."

"I've always favored the term concubine."

"And I've always favored the term eunuch, if you get my drift. Regardless, I can try to handle some stuff from my end. I'll kick a few teeth in for show, that'll slow things down. I can also keep sowing bullshit for you. Before he left, James shared with me a few extra tidbits about Freewills from our archives. Not much, mind you. Most of this shit is above even his pay grade. But enough that I can maybe spin a few more stories."

"Have you heard from him?"

"Nope."

That sucked. James was in charge of all vampire covens in the Northeast, a powerhouse of a vamp over five hundred years old. He was also a pretty cool dude from what I'd seen, which seemed to be a rarity among the undead. He could have ended this nonsense with a single appearance. Sadly, he'd been called away to Asia by his superiors. There was no telling when he'd be back and his stand-in, Colin, wasn't the type to give low-level schlubs like me any help at all.

"You think anyone will make a move against us?"

"Definitely a possibility."

"Dusk Reaper?"

She rolled her eyes at that. "Not at first. He's older than me, but too much of a coward deep down to try anything unless he thinks the others will back him up. The real danger is going to be if he can convince folks like Dread Stalker and Victor. They're a lot tougher than him and they know how to fight."

Uh, yeah. Goddamn. I really needed to take notes on who was sticking with their stupid coven names and who was dropping them.

"That's the bigger problem. If that happens, they might decide to move on us in force. If so, we are fucked with a capital F."

"So how do we rein things in?"

"*We* don't. You do. Like it or not, Bill, you're gonna have to do something to earn back their respect. Believe me when I say our lives depend on it."

I needed time to think. It looked like most of the coven had departed for the evening to go about their own business, probably killing the shit out of people to spite the rules I'd recently laid down. That was fine by me – them being gone, not the killing people part. Sally was encouraging me to pick one of them as a sacrificial lamb and then ice their ass with extreme prejudice in a way the others would be able to respect. Sadly for us, I wasn't particularly big on the idea of casual murder, not even if the person was a monumental asshole.

I also wasn't entirely certain I could pull it off. I was easily the youngest vampire in the coven. Youngest equaled weakest for the undead. Sure, I might have more strength than a bodybuilder, but human standards didn't really apply in this case. By vamp standards I was ... well, what I'd been for most of my life: a pudgy guy with very little muscle tone.

Sally had finally stopped badgering me when I promised to come up with something. Though I was loathe to admit it, she had a point. Having seen enough vampires in action, I knew that talk was cheap among their kind. They'd kill a person or another vamp without a moment's hesitation. I still wasn't certain whether living for all eternity appealed to me or not, but I had to admit I definitely didn't relish the prospect of dying young.

If there was an easy answer to all of this, it eluded me. What could I do that wouldn't end with me either as a pile of ashes or having turned into an icy-blooded sociopath like the rest of them?

Go figure. On a night when my only plan had been to find a few pairs of tits on pay cable, I'd somehow stepped into a heaping pile of bullshit instead. Sadly, the suckage of the evening wasn't quite finished with me yet.

On the way home, I racked my brain for a good hour, but couldn't come up with jack or shit. Unfortunately, the whole mess had me so distracted that I ended up missing my fucking transfer.

I ended up sitting on the A train for several more stops than I'd intended, taking me into Queens. That was verboten territory as it was home to the HBC and they weren't overly fond of me at the moment.

It was late, though, and I didn't feel like hanging around and being accosted for change while I waited for the train on the opposite track. The beauty of vampire physiology is that distances which might be worth a cab ride for a human are a pretty easy run for a vamp. Considering the late hour, I figured I'd have a pretty good chance of walking into my apartment sooner if I made the journey on foot. All in all, it seemed worth the risk.

As it turns out, much like so many other items that night, I was wrong.

5

FEAR NOT, GOOD CITIZEN

For a long time, the unofficial credo attributed to New Yorkers had been "I don't want to get involved." This was all thanks to a well-publicized murder from the 1960's. Most of us like to think that when shit is going down, we'll react in a way that would make our mothers proud. In reality, oftentimes putting one's fingers in one's ears and going "la la la" is the easier course. The thing is, occasionally it's the wiser one as well.

Sadly, much like the elven battlemage I play at my weekly D&D game, I wasn't known for my wisdom.

I'd gone a few blocks at most, the empty streets zipping by in the darkness as I put my speed to good use, when I heard the cry.

It had been faint, easy to miss even in a slumbering city, but my hearing was several times sharper than a normal person's. Despite my intent to get home and kick my roommates awake so as to brainstorm a solution to my problems, I stopped and listened. The cry came again, followed by the sharp bark of what sounded like a small dog. Had someone's Pomeranian gotten loose and was, even now, rampaging through the streets while its hapless owner chased after it?

Oh well, that wasn't my problem. Stupid fucking rat dogs. I was about to ignore it and continue on my way when my overly sensitive ears picked up another voice – this one low, barely audible even to me.

"Scream all you want, bitch."

That stopped me dead in my tracks. A smart person would have dialed 911. Hell, a smart vampire would too, right before getting the fuck out of there. Not that I believed in playing to stereotypes, but I probably didn't look like the type who'd be wandering these streets alone at this time. The last thing I needed was a suspicious cop thinking I was a meth-head out looking to score.

It was the small part of me enamored with being a vampire that ultimately decided to pursue what was surely an insane course of action. That's the thing about waking up one day with super powers. It tends to dull our logic circuits while automatically making us believe in our own invincibility. Of course, it's that kind of bullshit reasoning that makes people sew up a homemade Batman costume only to end up in the morgue by day's end.

Damn my sense of social responsibility! Despite knowing the monumental stupidity of what I was about to do, I homed in on the direction of the voices and took off at full speed – hoping to not become yet another sad statistic in a city with far too many.

I glanced around the corner and saw them. Two men, both of average height, stood over their victim an old woman, her brown skin covered in wrinkles, easily seventy, maybe more. She was sitting with her back against the alley wall, holding her little dog protectively. The mutt looked small enough to fit inside a hamster cage. As far as protection went, one would've been hard pressed to pick a more useless theft deterrent. The little rodent let out a warning bark every few seconds, but even it seemed to sense how idle its threats were.

This was all happening between two rundown apartment complexes. It didn't take a genius to figure out what had transpired. Apparently granny there had decided to take Fido for a walk, lest the little beast piss her rug again. Sadly, she'd picked a night when there were predators about.

A small part of me wondered where the cops were. The old woman's cries had fallen silent, no doubt under threat from the two goons accosting her, but the dog's shrill yips were plenty loud in the narrow confines of the space.

Almost as if in answer to my unasked question, a voice came from above. "Shut the fuck up!" The sound of a window slamming shut followed a moment later.

Such a wonderful neighborhood.

"You heard the man, bitch," one of the assailants said, his voice betraying a slight Latino lilt. He picked up a discarded flashlight, probably the old lady's, and threw it against the wall where it shattered. "Shut your fucking dog up. Or better yet, we will."

The woman shrank back even further, cradling the dog to her like it was a child. Hell, the little rodent probably was to her. When she spoke, her voice was low and pleading. "Please don't hurt Mr. Piddles. I gave you my purse, that's all I have."

Mr. Piddles?

The two men chuckled and then the other answered, "We don't want your purse, you old bag. We want you."

Oh, crap. So much for this being a simple mugging. What is it with the sick fucks in this world? Had this merely been an altercation over a few dollars, I might still have minded my own business. Now, though, shit was about to get serious. It was time to show these assholes that there were darker things afoot this night.

I took a moment to pull the hood of my light jacket up over my head, taking a cue from Bruce Willis in *Unbreakable*. Too bad for these fuckheads that they were both about to audition for the role of Mr. Glass.

That done, I let loose with all my speed – racing to their position before they could make good on their threats. I put my head down and shoulder-tackled the first, sending him flying into his friend. It was a hit that would have gotten me a first round draft pick as an NFL linebacker had any scouts been present. Sadly, such a career change seemed unlikely, so I had to take satisfaction at seeing the two dick-wads go tumbling head over heels to land in a heap.

Taking a moment to enjoy my handiwork, I turned toward the old lady – her eyes now wide circles of white in the dark alleyway. I'd probably appeared so fast that she didn't have a clue what was happening.

"It's okay." I held out a hand to her. "You're safe..."

"Well, well, seems we got ourselves a fucking hero here."

Guess I spoke too soon. I glanced over, wondering if maybe the assholes had backup. Instead, I saw them both up on their feet. What the fuck? I'd hit them hard enough to easily crack bone. The only way these guys should have been standing was after a long stay in the hospital followed by weeks of physical therapy. Yet they appeared unhurt. Either these guys were really good actors, I was a lot less tough than I thought, or...

That "or" part was confirmed when the first one smiled in my direction. The expression held no mirth to it. It was the look of someone who knew some-thing the other didn't. A moment later I was clued in as I watched his canines elongate. Fuck me. What were the chances I'd run into a couple of HBC vamps?

Actually, considering they were right in front of me, probably one-hundred percent.

Just wonderful. I'd been paddling down shit's creek all night and now I'd just turned a bend and spotted rapids ahead.

Thankfully it was too dark for the old lady to see much – aside from maybe her attackers not being out of the fight yet. That in of itself was bad enough. Had she possessed night vision like me and seen that she was now in the presence of monsters, I can't help but think that might have sent her off the deep end.

"Don't you fucking move," the second attacker, an ugly guy with pockmarked skin and a shaved head, told the old woman. Much to my annoyance, she shrank back and obeyed. Hell, I couldn't even get my former college girlfriend to do that when she was shit-faced drunk.

"It'll be all right," I whispered to her, although I had to imagine how lame that sounded. Hell, I was having a hard time convincing myself. Ending up the meat in a beat-down sandwich didn't seem like a particularly wonderful way to end my evening.

"So, hero," the first one said mockingly, "you want to put on your cape and fly now? No? Maybe you want to try running then? Go ahead. Try it."

Hmm, obviously these guys thought I was just some random Good Samaritan. Still, I seriously considered doing as he said. As young as I was, I had little doubt putting on a burst of vampire speed would surprise them long enough for me to get my ass to safety.

But then I glanced over and saw the old lady, still cowering with her pet squirrel. I knew now this wasn't a simple robbery. These were vampires and they were out hunting. It was a fair bet they weren't here to recruit either. They'd drain her dry and then leave her for the rats. Fuck me and my sense of decency, but I couldn't allow that.

Instead of doing the smart thing, I said, "I don't run from asses. I kick them."

I faced them down and bared my fangs, hoping maybe the presence of another vamp might cause them to back off. How and why that would work – I had no idea, but hope was a fool's errand anyway and I was apparently quite the fool.

At the very least, it caused them to hesitate for a second, just long enough for me to realize it was time to put up or shut up. During my first few weeks as a vamp, Sally had imparted upon me the necessity of appearance in the world of the undead. I'd taken it to heart then, but I'll be the first to admit I'd let it lapse in the months since I'd taken the top spot. It was time to relearn that lesson all over again.

I took a step forward, feigning confidence I didn't feel, trying to psych myself out by remembering that these two might be vampires, but they were still big enough pussies that they felt the need to gang up on a feeble old woman. The thought – asshole predators singling out the old and weak – pissed me off and I used that anger as an anchor to keep myself from doing the smart thing and turning tail.

"Who the fuck are you?" the first guy asked. "This is our territory. The HBC don't like no..."

"You know damn well who I am, shithead," I snarled. "Some of your friends met me a few months back. They didn't really enjoy that. I don't think you will either."

"Oh, shit, man," Baldy said. "No fucking way. You're that Freewill freak."

I gave a mock bow. "I see my reputation precedes me." Thank God for a semester of drama club at NJIT.

"You killed Big Mike," the first one said. "He was my friend, motherfucker."

I'd done nothing of the sort. The Howard Beach Coven had been caught recruiting above their quota and James had culled their excess numbers as a lesson to them. Unfortunately, I'd somehow gotten stuck with the tab. Sadly, placing the blame on someone who wasn't there probably wasn't my ticket to getting out of this mess. "Maybe you need to make better friends."

"Or maybe we need to bring your ass back to Samuel. Bet he'd reward us real good."

Oh fuck. Samuel was the HBC's master. From what I'd heard, he was two hundred years old, tough as nails, and had a major chip on his shoulder. That he also blamed me for the deaths of his coven members made it a fair bet that any meeting between us wouldn't involve hugs, pats on the back, or even a friendly reach around.

That sealed it. I either had to win this fight or hope for a really quick and preferably painless death.

6

HOLDING OUT FOR A HERO

The only tactical advantage in my favor was the narrowness of the alley. It wouldn't be easy for anyone to get past me and gain flank. If that happened, well, one didn't need to be versed in D&D rules to know that was a bad thing.

My only hope was to win this and I didn't think talking would get that shit done. Sadly, I was probably going to have to cross the line between my humanity and becoming one with the creature I'd tried to deny. In short, I was going to have to dust these fuckers. I just didn't know if I could actually bring myself to do it.

While I was contemplating this existential crisis, they both rushed me. Seeing them cross the distance between us with frightful speed made my choice seem much more palatable. The skinhead went low, while his Latin friend took the high road. Reacting out of pure instinct alone, I leapt – using every ounce of strength in my legs to propel me upward.

I almost made it too. The first fuckhead missed me completely and went sailing past. Sadly, I caught his friend on the face on the way up. I took some satisfaction in the crunch my sneaker made against his nose right before I went pinwheeling through the air.

Through some miracle of luck, I landed on top of the guy who'd just gotten a mouthful of Adidas. He might've been older and tougher, but never discount being on the wrong end of an impact. I nearly brained myself in the process, but the pained grunt he made told me I'd knocked the wind out of him.

A memory stirred within me of my first encounter with the HBC from months back and I knew what needed to be done if I were to have any chance of surviving the night. Still woozy from the fall, I grabbed the nearest appendage to my sprawled form – his leg – and bit into it with everything I had.

Real life vampires are tough, but there are downsides. Sunlight is one of them. What most don't realize, though, is that blood can be another. Sure, vamps feed upon humans and dig the taste of blood, but there's a caveat – it has to be the blood of the living. If a regular vamp tries to bite down on another, regardless of whether it's during kinky *True Blood* sex or not, they're gonna end the evening puking their guts out as if they'd just spent the weekend in Tijuana drinking from random faucets.

I'm not a regular vampire, though. My unique nature affords me a few perks, the best being that vamp blood doesn't give me the Hershey squirts. Quite the contrary. I not only can handle it, I actually thrive on that shit. When I chow down on another vampire, I somehow temporarily ingest their power as well.

The effect is not unlike adding nitrous to a car engine for a quick supercharge. That feeling hit my stomach as I tore into the HBC vamp's calf muscle and sucked down his blood as if my life depended on it.

My victim struggled against me, but I had the advantage of leverage. Alas, he had the advantage of having brought a friend. Thankfully, rather than stake me in the back like a smart opponent, strong hands grabbed hold of my jacket and tore me away from the other vampire. He dragged me off and threw me down the alley; I sailed a good fifteen feet before hitting the unyielding concrete.

Too bad for the skinhead vamp, he was too little and too late in coming to the rescue. I landed, skidded, and then rolled back to my feet – feeling the lacerations on my hands and knees already beginning to knit themselves back together thanks to the power boost I'd just gotten.

Skinhead helped his buddy back to his feet. His friend now sported a nasty limp courtesy of my fangs. Oh well, fuck him. I still had the taste of his leg in my mouth and, believe me, this was one asshole who could've done with a long shower.

I'd managed to even the odds a bit, but that was a long way from winning. The two HBC vamps hesitated, more wary this time, but I didn't fool myself into thinking the rest of this fight would be easy. I scanned the alley for something I could use, but spied nothing except some random garbage. I had a feeling that beating them off with a discarded six pack carton wouldn't do much, unless they were maybe really into recycling. Looking back their way, I saw the situation had gotten even worse. Both vamps reached into their jackets and produced weapons: a box cutter for the first and a wicked hunting knife for the ugly bald one.

Shit!

They came at me again. The first vamp limped for a few steps, but then his healing must've kicked in as he quickly accelerated. The bald-headed one, wise to my trick from their first assault, waited for a moment then tensed his legs and leapt, clearing ten feet into the air as he held his blade aloft – looking to sink it somewhere nice and soft, like me.

His buddy reached me first and took a swing with the razor. Sadly for him, he wasn't well versed on his Freewill lore. I caught his arm mid-swing then fell back and dragged him with me, just as his buddy came down on us with the knife.

Though the razor in the first vamp's hands sliced me on the shoulder, I barely felt it. Besides, it was nothing compared to the six inches of steel that sank between his shoulder blades – his friend being unable to halt his momentum.

I landed on my ass and then watched, stunned, as a flash of light erupted from the first vampire's chest. In the space of a second, he immolated from the inside out. It was only by luck that I managed to close my mouth before the rain of hot ash that resulted washed down upon me.

Holy crap.

I stared wide-eyed up at the second vamp, standing there still holding his knife, but apparently in an equal amount of shock.

I'd just killed a vampire. Well, okay, his friend had done the deed, but I'd dragged the guy in front of me, purposely putting him in the path of the fatal blow.

I wasn't sure whether to laugh or puke as I contemplated the life I'd just snuffed out. Sadly, this was a bad time to freak. I still had one more vamp to deal with and he was both armed and likely to be pissed about his buddy. He seemed to realize it too as our eyes met and a snarl erupted from his throat.

He raised the knife high ... and that was when the old lady found her voice again and started screaming. Go figure – being assaulted, saved, and then witnessing a fight that ended with one of the combatants exploding into ash had probably unnerved her ever so slightly.

The HBC vamp hesitated as her shrill cry cut through the night air. Within seconds more voices, angry tenants no doubt, joined in from above.

"Shut the fuck up!"

"I have to work in the morning!"

"That's it. I'm calling the fucking cops!"

That last one seemed to get through to my opponent and he took a step back. Uncertainty filled his eyes. He was no doubt debating the odds. Could he take me before the cops got there? If not, could he take me and the cops at the same time? Apparently the answer was no, as he looked down at me, spat, and then took off down the alley – his vampiric speed ensuring he was gone before I had a chance to utter, "And don't come back."

Unfortunately, if the cops were on their way – probably a big *if,* all things considered – that meant I needed to make my ass scarce too. First things first, though. One doesn't save a victim and then take off before ensuring said victim is all right. That wouldn't be cool.

Picking myself up, I dusted the last of the dead HBC vamp off me – again trying not to think about what I'd just done – and walked over to where the old lady still cowered.

Her eyes widened as I approached and her little dog, no doubt sensing its master's fright, began to growl in my direction. I held up my hands to hopefully show I meant no harm.

"It's okay. They're gone." I bent down and held out a hand for her.

"Who are you?" she asked, her voice a bare whisper.

"I'm..." Oh crap. I couldn't exactly give her my name. The last thing I wanted was for the cops to show up at my doorstep asking for a statement. Drawing attention to myself was a bad thing, especially since I had no alibi as to what the hell I was doing here at this time of night. I needed to make something up, but what? So I said the first thing that popped into my head.

I opened my mouth into a big friendly smile. "I'm Dr. Death."

In retrospect I should've considered two things: first off, Dr. Death isn't a particularly reassuring name to be giving old ladies at two AM in the fucking morning and I really need to remember to retract my fangs before grinning at people.

The combination set her off again and she erupted into screams of terror. Unfortunately, in doing so, she also let go of Mr. Piddles who—much like any good doggie—didn't waste any time in attacking me.

The little weasel latched onto one of my sneakers with a death grip, snarling like it was actually a threat to anything bigger than a slice of baloney.

"Hey, call off your..." And that's when I heard the whine of sirens in the distance. Shit! Of all the nights for the police to be responsive.

"Listen, lady..." I slipped and almost lost my footing as her attack rat refocused his teeth onto the cuff of my pants. "Seriously, you need to..." Fuck this shit! I kicked my leg out to dislodge the dog, forgetting for one wee moment that I currently possessed the combined strength of two vampires. The end result was a wet splatter as Mr. Piddles slammed into the side of the building at roughly the same speed as a Major League fastball. Oh crap!

Yeah, that definitely could have ended better.

7

ORIGIN STORY

Needless to say, granny didn't take the death of her beloved pet with a great deal of dignity. She began tearing at her hair. All the while, her screams rose in intensity until I was sure my ears would bleed.

That was it. No fucking way did I have any chance of making this right – at least not before the cops showed up and busted my ass for animal cruelty.

Unable to think of something more profound to say than, "Sorry," I took off, quickly accelerating to full speed as I attempted to put this encounter far behind me.

By that point I no longer had any shits left to give. Pulling my hood tighter around my head on the off chance that any red light cameras happened to catch my speeding form, I kept going until I was only a few blocks from home. Only then did I slow down to a more human pace as I walked the final distance to my building.

I climbed the stairs to the top floor, let myself into the dark apartment, and made my way to my bedroom where hopefully I'd be able to convince myself that this had all been a bad dream.

Sleep eluded me for the rest of the night. I ended up lying in bed and staring at the ceiling as I tried to make sense of what had happened. Oddly enough, the thing I felt worst about was the old lady's dog. Sure, I couldn't stand those little yippy pieces of shit, but that didn't mean I had meant to pop it like a water balloon. A part of me insisted I should have felt much worse about the vampire. I mean, he'd been a person. Maybe he had a family and ... well, okay, dickface hadn't exactly seemed the wife and two point five kids sort.

The problem was I couldn't quite get over the weirdness of how vampires kicked the bucket. It almost made them seem ... I dunno ... less real. That was stupid of course. *I* was a vampire and had little doubt that turning to dust was an unpleasant experience. Still, seasons of Buffy and multiple Blade movies had gone a long way toward ruining the emotional impact of ending a vampire life for me. And, in all fairness, it didn't help the guy's cause that he'd been a marauding asshole preying on a defenseless old lady. Live by the sword, die by the stake—or knife in this case.

Finally, morning arrived as evidenced by the light filtering through my closed blinds. Thankfully, another benefit of my physiology was the need for much less sleep than I'd previously required. Regardless, I wasn't exactly bouncing out of bed. I'd been told vampires have a natural proclivity toward being nocturnal – which made sense since direct sunlight could reduce us to a charred crisp faster than a burrito left in the microwave too long. It meant that no matter how much rest I got, I was always dragging my ass a bit during the day.

Oh well. Sadly for me, being turned hadn't meant an instant windfall of riches. I still had to work for a living. Even though my job allowed me to work remotely, that meant most days I needed to be awake during the time when other vamps would be nestled all cozy in their beds or filthy crypts. At least today was Sunday, which meant I could procrastinate getting up. Hell, any port in a storm.

After a while, I heard noises coming from the living room. Ed was out visiting his stepfather in Pennsylvania this weekend, which meant it had to be Tom. He worked in the Manhattan financial district, so was in the habit of getting up early most days – unless he was piss-faced drunk the night before. If he was up, it meant I hadn't missed any good parties while I'd been out playing coven stooge. It was a small victory, but I'd take it.

When I finally got my ass out of bed, I found him seated on our cheap-ass couch behind his laptop. Rather than the spreadsheets one might expect of a minion working his way up the corporate ladder, he was watching a cartoon in which a multi-tentacled demon fucked a wide-eyed anime girl in the ass—as well as pretty much every other hole. From the look of things, she had about forty feet worth of his appendages inside of her. Goddamn, the Japanese were weird.

I stepped up behind him and cleared my throat.

Tom glanced over his shoulder and asked, "S'up, Bill?" in between mouthfuls of Cookie Crisp.

"Really?" I asked. "What is it, like seven AM?"

"Don't judge."

"Too late." I glanced again at his screen. "Is that *Midnight Girl Oni?*"

"No. It's the sequel – *Midnight Girl Oni Returns.*"

"Don't think I've seen that one. Shoot me the link when you get the chance."

"No problem. Oh hey!" He paused the video. "I've got a bone to pick with you."

"Listen, man, I had a bit of a night and..."

"That can wait. You put blood in the fucking syrup bottle."

"So? Goes good on pancakes that way."

"First off, that's fucking gross. Secondly, I only found out because I tried using it earlier."

Oops. I really needed to remember to label my stuff. "Whatever the fuck. It was my syrup. I bought it."

"It doesn't work that way. Condiments are communal."

"Communal syrup? Since when?"

"Since always."

"If that's the case, then why did you flip the fuck out when I used your wasabi a few weeks back?"

"The rule doesn't apply to imported condiments. Everyone knows that."

I walked into the kitchen and got a pot of coffee brewing. "You are so full of shit."

"I don't make the rules, I just follow them."

"Can I pour some blood in my coffee, oh mighty one, or is it communal caffeine too?"

"Coffee is fine. Just don't put it directly in the pot."

"Asshole," I commented under my breath.

"So what happened?"

"Huh?" I asked, turning back toward him.

"You said you had a rough night."

"Oh yeah. You know the drill. I fucked Sally then she kept begging me for more. Bitch couldn't get enough."

Tom stood and walked to our kitchen nook with his empty cereal bowl. He gave it the most cursory of rinses in the sink, then put it back in the cabinet. "I asked what *you* did last night, not what Bizarro Bill did."

"It could happen." He continued to stare at me until I broke down and grinned. "Okay fine, but I'm serious. One day I'm gonna tap that tight little ass of hers."

"And should that happen, I shall raise a toast in your name ... probably posthumously."

"Yeah, but it'll be worth it."

I told Tom about my adventure from the night before. It took a while because he kept asking me to back up and fill in more details on Eliza. My dating life was pretty pathetic, but his wasn't any better and it showed. Oh well, at least desperation loved company.

"So you actually tried to save that old woman?" he asked with a slight hint of admiration to his voice. "That's pretty fucking cool."

I thought back to her dog. "Didn't quite work out that way."

"Fuck that noise, dude. The little fucking rat probably deserved it anyway."

I rubbed the bridge of my nose, feeling a stress headache coming on. Tom was my oldest friend, but unburdening my troubles on him was often not the most cathartic of exercises. "I didn't help her just to punt her dog into oblivion, dipshit. That sort of defeats the point. Fuck! I figured maybe I'd have one good thing come out of last night, but I had to fuck that up too. Now I have most of the goddamned coven looking to kill me, the HBC looking to kill me, and Sally who'll probably kill me if I don't find a way to fix this shit."

When I looked up again, my roommate was gone. He'd walked back to his laptop while I'd been ranting. "What the hell, man? Am I that fucking boring?"

"No ... well, normally you are," he said from over his shoulder, "but in this case it sounds like some real shit went down."

"So then what are...?"

"I'm checking out Google News."

"Why?"

"Did you not just listen to yourself? You went all Dark Knight on those HBC cocksuckers. I want to see if anyone picked up on the story. How fucking cool would that be?"

"I don't think Sally would find it all that cool. I'm not exactly supposed to go around shouting from the ramparts that vampires exist."

"This wouldn't be about vampires, stupid," he said dismissively. "All this happened in the middle of Queens. I bet some intrepid reporter slipped a cop a twenty, got the scoop, and wrote an awesome piece about..." He paused and turned to look at me. "Did you give the old lady a name?"

"My name?"

"Not your real name. Did you give her a code name?"

"Oh. Yeah. I gave her my coven name."

"You did not."

"It was all I could think of."

"Are you a fucking idiot? Nobody is gonna want to be saved by some psycho named Dr. Death. You should have come up with something better like the Shadow Warrior or Dark Justice..."

"I really didn't have time to put a great deal of thought into it."

"Oh well, fuck it. I'm sure the press will come up with something cool."

"For what?"

"For ... oh ... Houston, I think we have liftoff. Check it out, I think this one is about you."

"Really?" I stepped across the room, suddenly

curious to see what he was looking at. I had to admit a small part of me didn't exactly mind the concept of getting a little credit for stopping a potential murder.

Queens Woman Institutionalized After Claiming Monsters Killed Her Dog.

I grimaced at what I saw. "Not quite the headline I was hoping for."

"Yeah, but it's pretty cool anyway."

"They locked her up in a nut house."

"Who cares? Even Batman fucked up his maiden voyage."

"Maiden voyage? You're not suggesting..."

"Oh, yes I am." He turned and smiled broadly at me "This city is about to get its very first superhero and that hero is you, my friend."

8

UP, UP AND AWAY

"Are you a fucking retard? No, don't say anything. I'm pretty sure I already know the answer."

Tom closed his laptop and stood. I could see the same insane glimmer he usually got in his eyes when he'd collected some toy that he was certain was worth a fortune. Most of the time he was full of shit, but that didn't stop him from becoming obsessive. "Think about it. It's perfect."

"No..."

"You have actual super powers."

"I'm not listening."

"The night is a second home to you."

"Not happening."

"And you already have the motivation."

I was about to turn and march back into my bedroom, but I stopped and asked, "Wait, what motivation?"

"Everyone in the coven wants to kill your ass."

"I'm well aware of that, thank you. I'm not sure how saving one little old lady is gonna solve that ... unless you think I should have fed her to them."

"Well, that might have helped."

I let out a sigh and turned around again, at which point he quickly added, "But that's not what I'm talking about."

"I know what you're talking about. You want me to dress up in a cape and skulk along the rooftops so you can live out some sick masturbatory superhero fantasy vicariously through me. Well, no dice. I'm not one of your fucking action figures."

"No, but technically you do owe me a replacement for Opti..."

"Can we please stop talking about that?" I gritted my teeth at the memory. That stupid toy, which had somehow gotten infused with magic and become the equivalent of a holy hand grenade. Sure, it had proven helpful against Jeff, but fuck me if my roommate hadn't whined continually about it ever since.

"Do you know how much that thing was worth?"

I rounded on Tom, blackening my eyes in the process. "Yes I do! I looked it up in fact. Not nearly as much as you fucking make it out to be."

"Now maybe, but in the future..." One of his eyebrows rose quizzically as he stared at me. "By the way, what are you doing?"

In an attempt to look intimidating and maybe get him to back off, I'd raised my hands and extended my claws ... or tried to. Glancing at them, I saw that rather than wicked talons, my fingernails had maybe grown a quarter of an inch. "Shit."

"Still haven't figured that out, have you?"

"There isn't exactly a manual for these things."

"Sally?"

"She keeps telling me to stop bothering her and just go fucking practice."

"I'd say you need more."

"No shit, Sherlock." I blinked a few times. "Are my eyes back to normal?"

"Looks like it."

At least I'd gotten that part down fairly well. If I ever decided to go to a Comic-Con and cosplay as Riddick from *Pitch Black* I'd be all set.

"See?" Tom asked, a smile on his face. "This is exactly why my plan is so perfect."

Realizing I wasn't going to be left alone until he said his piece, I relented. "Okay, fine. Explain why pretending to be some Moon Knight knockoff is gonna help me."

"For starters, it's gonna give you some practice. I think your problem is you're thinking too hard about it and also you really don't want to hurt me."

"Oh?"

"Yeah, I'm far too awesome. But in the heat of battle when some asshole is coming after you, you're the only hope the orphans and the hot school teacher charged with their protection have, I have no doubt..."

"Wait, where did the orphans come from?"

"I'm just illustrating a scenario here. Can you please shut the fuck up and let me finish? Good. Anyway, think about it. You'd be a natural. You heal like Wolverine. You have claws like Sabretooth..."

"Sabretooth is a bad guy."

"Not in Age of Apocalypse."

"Point taken."

"And you're as strong as Captain America. That screams hero potential to me. But, here's the best part. You're not going to be out there hunting criminals."

"I'm not? But you said..."

"Use your brain for a second, Bill. Think of how fucking boring that would be. You got lucky last night and stumbled upon that shit, but imagine how many hours Batman must spend standing atop some spire somewhere, scratching his ass through his bat-suit, and hoping someone gets mugged. The comics make it look like Spider-man can't take a shit without Carnage climbing up his ass, but in real life interesting stuff doesn't happen every day ... unless your quest for justice involves helping the cops sort out fender benders."

I was still stuck on Tom's definition of lucky, but he did have a point about the rest. A real life super-hero would probably end up bored out of his fucking mind without a flashing red phone or bat signal to tell him when shit was going down. "Okay, I get what you're saying, but then what's the point of all this if I'm not going to hunt..."

"Vampires."

"Huh?"

"You're going to hunt vampires."

"I'm pretty sure the folks up in Boston would take exception to one of their coven masters deciding to go all Van Helsing on his own troops." Or then again, maybe not. I still wasn't certain on the rules about these things.

"That's fine ... it's also irrelevant. See, you're not going to be killing vampires. You're going to be saving people from them."

"What's the difference? More importantly, how does that help me at all?"

Tom gave a pained sigh as he plopped back down onto the couch. "Need I explain everything? You're a vampire. You know of two other covens of vampires in the area. Hell you're in charge of one of them, right?"

"True."

"Let's forget about the Howard Beach vamps for the moment. They're tough, they've got street cred. Sounds like there's a better chance of them kicking your ass. However, you said it yourself, your coven is mostly a bunch of supermodels and long-haired pretty boys. Although on that first part, I need to reiterate the fact that you coming home to Ed and me every day makes me seriously doubt your sexual preferences."

"Get to the point or I'm gonna find a lot more than syrup to mix my blood in with."

"I'm getting there. You told those frat house vamps to stop hunting people, but haven't enforced that rule in a way they respect. Is that correct?"

"In a nutshell."

"So, you know what they look like and you know where they hunt. Concentrate your stakeouts in those places. When you see one leading an unwary victim away, you swoop down…"

"Swoop?"

"Or climb down, or fall on your fucking face. It doesn't matter. You jump in, kick the shit out of them, and then make your escape. Do it enough times and your reputation ... or your alter ego's anyway will grow."

I thought about that for a moment. He did have a point. When I'd first been turned, I was scared shit-less. I mean, waking up in a den of monsters was not how I'd intended to end that night. But then I learned a few things. For starters, once the coven found out I was a Freewill, a good chunk of them stopped harassing me. Turns out that most predators are only brave when their prey is weak. Add in an unknown element and they'll act like kids, afraid to turn off the closet light at night. I was living proof of that ... or had been. Seems I'd gone to that well one too many times and come back with nothing but a bucket of sand. I expressed as much to Tom.

"That's the beauty of it. You'll scare the fuck out of those vamps. But then, when you're hanging out with the coven, you'll be all brave and shit. You'll tell those pussies to man the fuck up and show them you're not afraid of some vigilante vampire hunter. After a while we'll stage something ... maybe throw Ed in the costume and let you beat the snot out of him in front of witnesses. Before you know it, you'll be back on top. Your coven will think you're awesome for stepping up."

"And I'll really save some people in the process?"

"Yeah, that too."

Holy shit. He actually had some good points. I

needed to mark this occasion down somewhere. Usually Tom was the type to talk me into stupid shit, like that time in college I chugged a liter of Everclear. But this ... it had potential. "Do you really think it could work?"

"Like a charm, my friend. Hell, maybe you'll even get a couple of decent headlines written about you."

9

THE BIRTH OF A LEGEND

I know how these things go. I've seen *Kick-Ass* enough times to know that going out unprepared on your first patrol can lead to some serious hurt.

Tom and I spent that entire day making a list of things that needed to be taken care of.

A costume itself was easy. Thank goodness for the internet and next day shipping. After a couple hours of surfing the web, including some fetish shops, I decided that rather than become Gimp Man, I'd go with something more down to Earth. We're talking black clothing, a trench coat, and a full-visor motorcycle helmet. Think *The Matrix* meets *The Wraith*. I ended up balking at the cost of actual body armor, but Tom solved that ... sorta.

"You want me to wear baking pans under my shirt?"

"They're metal aren't they? They just need to work

good enough to keep any pointy objects out of your heart."

I doubted his logic there, but my bank account said that compromises needed to be made so I said a silent prayer that the Pillsbury Dough Boy would keep me safe and we moved on.

Weaponry was a must. After all, the vamps of Village Coven were older than me and it would be a dead giveaway if I had to resort to biting them. Thankfully that was easy to figure out. Vamps might be tough, but blunt force trauma was a pretty good equalizer. Some of what we wanted couldn't be shipped to New York thanks to the state's stupid laws, but fortunately my parents lived in Jersey and they didn't ask questions.

Speaking of vampires, though, there was also smell to take into consideration. I wasn't sure if a vamp could tell another by scent – I wasn't experienced enough to know for certain – but with our enhanced noses it seemed likely. I thought that could be an issue, but then Tom picked up the phone.

"Who are you calling?"

"Ed. His old man is a survival nut."

"I wouldn't go that far."

"The shotgun under Ed's bed says different. Needless to say, he lives in the sticks and owns lots of firearms. Close enough for me."

A few minutes later, Tom got off the phone, having secured that Ed's stepdad did indeed have some scent killing shit to throw off deer and that he would be bringing a bottle of it back with him upon his return.

"No questions asked?"

Tom smiled. "'Tis one of the perks of having a bloodsucker for a roommate. One learns to accept the weird and unusual with but a shrug and acceptance."

"Think he'll try to talk us out of this?"

Tom and I looked at each other for a moment before bursting out laughing. Who was I kidding? This was the same roommate who'd stabbed me with a knife to prove to Tom that I was undead. Hell, he'd probably want to videotape the whole fucking thing for posterity's sake.

The beauty of my *arrangement* with Sally was that it took into account my day job and anything else I did in my sad quest to have a life. Also, she liked that I typically only showed up on weekends because it allowed her to run things as she pleased, without any of my pesky morality around to muck things up.

This time around, though, I had a feeling it was gonna be rougher on her than usual. She had a lot of damage control to do. I kinda felt bad leaving it up to her. I mean, she was only one vampire. Even she couldn't keep eyes in the back of her head twenty-four/seven. In essence, I was leaving her to clean up my mess. I still wasn't sure of my feelings for Sally. On the one hand, she was a total self-absorbed bitch. On the other, she'd gone out on a limb for me more than once. I wasn't quite sure if I was ready to extend the title of friend to her, but she was definitely more than a casual acquaintance. Regardless, I didn't relish the thought of anything happening to her while I was off tending to my day job and pretending that I still had a heartbeat.

Thankfully that didn't look to be the case for long. Though it pained my wallet to do so, the expedited shipping of my supplies meant that the wait was fairly short. As expected, Ed was full on in, handing out a rare compliment to Tom for coming up with the idea and jumping in with his own suggestions.

Come the end of that week we were ready to put our plan into motion.

"Can you come in here?"

"What?"

I raised my voice to make sure it was heard outside the helmet. "I said, get your ass in here!" Maybe if a 2.0 update was needed to my vigilante costume, we could spring for a Bluetooth speaker or something. Thankfully, the vamps whom I'd be targeting had damned good hearing.

"I'm on the phone."

"Well hang up. You spend too much on sex hotlines as it is."

"Hold on a sec."

Muffled though my voice might be, I could still hear fine. Tom said his goodbyes to someone along with what sounded like ... nah, I must've been hearing wrong. It sounded like he said he'd see the other party soon. Odd. As far as I knew he had no plans to visit his parents.

"Dude," my roommate said, stepping to my doorway. "I'm trying to get a fucking date here. What the hell ... whoa."

I stood there, decked out in full battle gear. "How do you like it?"

"Pretty fucking badass."

I turned to the mirror and had to agree. Though I definitely didn't look like I was packing a superhero physique, the layers of clothing gave me a bulky look – and not just around the middle. The blackness of everything really helped too: from the combat boots, the trench coat, the helmet, and even the gloves– atop which I wielded a pair of brass knuckles that we'd spray painted to match the rest.

"How do you feel in it?"

"It should be fine unless we get a heat wave anytime soon." The baking pans I'd rigged to cover the front and back of my chest weren't the most comfortable things, but the bulky black sweater did a good job of hiding it in the front and it was pretty much invisible from the rear under the trench coat. Still felt like a dumb idea, but if it kept me from lining the bottom of an ashtray then it was worth it.

"Cool. Show Ed yet?"

"Yeah," I replied, taking off the helmet. "He came in earlier and hosed me down with that de-scenting shit."

"What did he think?"

"Said I'd be lucky to not be shot by a cop the second I step outside."

"Sounds like an endorsement to me. Oh hey, I've been thinking of a name."

"Oh god..."

"How about the Night Stalker?"

"Pretty sure that was a TV show."

"Fine. Just the Stalker then."

"Makes me sound like a rapist."

"We can use that." He put his hands on his hips and lowered his voice. "Fear not, for I am the Stalker, and I'm here to rape crime in the ass."

"Yeah, let's not go with that. It sounds ... wait, back up a second, did you say a date?"

"Fuck yeah! There's this new girl in our PR department. I've been passing her in the hall the last couple of days, giving her my winning smile."

"And she didn't immediately file a restraining order?"

"Fuck no. She actually asked me out to lunch today. Yeah, I know. Surprised the shit out of me too. So I'm trying to set something up. With any luck, I'll be fucking the daylights out of her before the weekend is through."

"And they say romance is dead. What if I need you, though? This is our big test run."

Tom placed a hand on my shoulder and looked me in the eye. "I know, and normally I'd be the Robin to your Batman ... not the fruity one in the panty-hose, mind you."

"For which I am grateful, don't get me wrong. What ever happened to bros before hoes, though?"

"It's still in effect."

"But?"

"*But* it's been a long time since I got my dick wet and some things have to be given priority."

Oddly enough, I couldn't really argue with that logic.

10

OUT ON PATROL

I realized, standing there in the alleyway watching Firebird work her charms on an unsuspecting fellow, that communicators were a definite plot crutch for comic book heroes. Seems they were always able to instantly talk to their teammates without any problems at all.

Being that I didn't own any Star Trek tech or even a decent headset, I had to rely on my cell phone – talking low so as to not be overheard by any vampire ears.

"I think she's making her move."

"Describe her," Tom said. His date had apparently come to her senses and rescheduled, much to his chagrin.

"It's that hot redhead I was telling you about."

"The one that Douche Razor was porking?"

"Thanks for reminding me."

"No problem. Just don't do anything yet."

"Why not?" I asked.

"Wait to see what she does. Maybe you can catch her in the middle of fucking him, see some tits."

"Give me that!" my other roommate, Ed, said from the other end of the connection. "You two really make me wonder if we're all the same species here."

"Bill isn't," Tom replied from the background.

"Fuck you, asshole," I spat into the receiver before looking up and seeing the two disappear inside the building they'd been conversing in front of. Her destination was obvious. The coven owned a small apartment on 20th, specifically designed for situations such as these: heavily soundproofed, vacancies on either side despite this being the middle of the city, high grade laminate flooring for easy cleanup ... that sort of thing. It was a place where a vamp could take their sweet time, as opposed to a quick alleyway feeding. That meant Firebird had plans for this guy.

I considered Tom's words. He was probably right. I had little doubt there'd be some boning going on in the short term. Firebird, no doubt named for her hair – real genius Jeff was, let me tell you – practically oozed sex with every step she took. She was the type, had she been human, who would have collected rich boyfriends like Tom collected action figures. Mind you, other than some flirting and a lot of blue-balling, none of that shit had ever come my way, but I digress.

Regardless of how the evening started for her *date*, it would end with him being carted out the back wrapped in plastic and destined to be forever remembered as a missing person. Or at least that's how she was planning it. My goal was to make sure things ended a wee bit differently.

As I crossed the street, just a guy wearing a black trench coat and carrying a duffel bag, I felt a twinge of guilt. Growing up, I'd been taught that it was not cool to hit women. Picking on those weaker than you was for the realm of the truly pathetic. Still, I needed to remember that the rules went out the window where the undead were concerned. A weak looking façade meant nothing. One needed to only look at Sally to see that. She was half my size, yet could have wiped the floor with me.

If anything, I was the disadvantaged party here. Still, we'd purposely chosen Firebird as my first target. She was a known hunter, flaunting my rules even before the coven had lost respect for me. However, she was far from being considered the crème de la crème of our fighters. I'd once heard Sally say, in a moment of cattiness, that Firebird could suck the skin off a cucumber but would still lose in a battle of wits to one.

Yeah, I was picking a comparatively easy mark for my first mission. Sue me. Even Spider-man started off with the regular Joe who iced his Uncle Ben before moving up to the Green Goblin.

I let myself into the building, noting the lobby was quiet. Another advantage of this place, so I'd been told, was all of the security cameras were dummies – fakes to make the real tenants feel safe, while at the same time letting the building's owners continue to be cheap fucks. Regardless, I waited until I got into the stairwell to unzip my bag and don my helmet, gloves, and baseball bat – also painted black ... gotta stick with a theme y'know.

Then, feeling like a reject from a *Mad Max* movie, I made my way up to the fifth floor. It was time to get this party started.

Tom and I had spent hours debating catch phrases or snippy one-liners. Never let it be said that we skimped on the important details. In the end, though, we decided ... well, okay, Ed decided after declaring every single thing I said to be pathetic ... that silence would say the most. I could see his point. What's more terrifying, some dude yelling "Flame on!" or being accosted by a silent vigilante – one who gives you no clue as to his motivation, other than your pain?

Yeah, I could dig that.

Or hopefully I could. My tongue sometimes had a mind of its own.

I stepped out into the hall and made my way to apartment 5-13, inwardly groaning at the clichéd choice in numbers. Sometimes the forces of darkness could be so predictable. I stepped in front of the door and readied myself. My delay was twofold in nature. This was my make it or break it moment. As for the rest, I knew the locks on the door were heavy duty. That was fairly common for coven properties. No point in trapping a human inside someplace they could easily escape from.

Even so, as a programmer I was well versed in the KISS method ... keep it simple, stupid. That meant always trying the obvious stuff before automatically assuming things were complicated. So, just for shits and giggles, I tested the door knob.

To my amazement, it turned. Talk about sloppy. I mean seriously, this was how the coven conducted business? Who the fuck doesn't lock...

Sadly, I stood there for a second too long gawking at the inept security. Maybe I'd made a noise or the latch clicking open alerted her, but either way the knob was yanked out of my hand as the door was pulled open from the inside.

"You guys know I'm using the apartment tonight so fuck..." the words died in Firebird's throat. From her indignation, she'd no doubt thought another coven member was infringing on her space. In a sense that was true, just not how she'd envisioned it. Anyway, apparently this chick had never gone to college. Everyone knows you're supposed to hang something on the doorknob to tell your roomies to take a hike when there's horizontal mambo lessons afoot. Jeez, did I have to explain everything to these dumbasses?

"Who the fuck are you?" she asked, regaining her composure.

Over her shoulder, I saw the guy she'd invited in. He was sitting on the couch looking impatient, his shirt already open in the front. He looked in my direction and stood. "You didn't tell me you had a roommate."

"She doesn't," I said, my voice low and threatening. So much for being the silent and deadly type.

I reared back a brass-knuckled fist, ready to deliver a haymaker to emphasize the point, but then I fucking hesitated. Though I knew damn well what she was, to my eyes Firebird still looked like a girl. I could hear my dad talking in my head telling me that only a fucking coward would do what I was about to – like I was some Joe Six-pack sitting around while my wife washed the laundry or did the dishes in a way that displeased my royal ass.

Sadly, the hesitation cost me. Firebird might not have had much of a rep as a brawler, but she was still a vampire. She grabbed me by the front of my sweat-shirt, her claws squealing against the metal tray covering my vitals, and dragged me bodily into the room – sending me flying into an end table.

Thanks, Dad!

I rolled with the landing, for the most part unhurt, but stayed down for a second longer than I needed to. First of all, I wanted to push any residual chivalrous bullshit to the back of my head and second, I realized she had no clue I was a vamp like her. My costume ... err uniform that is ... had worked. I could use that to my advantage.

"What, is it fucking Halloween already?" Firebird asked with a laugh as she turned and closed the door. This time she made it a point to latch the deadbolt, obviously thinking her intended snack was going to turn into an all you can eat special.

"What are you doing?" her date asked, showing that his end of the gene pool obviously hadn't been stirred with the clue stick.

"Sit down, lover. This is where it gets fun."

"I'm not into threesomes with other guys."

"Don't worry," I replied, lowering my voice an

octave and rising to my feet. "Someone is getting fucked here tonight, but it isn't you."

"What was that?"

Oh fuck me sideways with a rusty boat hook. "Never mind."

Firebird put her hands on her hips and laughed. "Let me help you out of that jacket and into something more comfortable, like your flayed skin." Really? She actually said that? I could see why she usually stuck to flirting. Sally's eyes would have practically rolled out of her head had she heard that line.

Firebird advanced upon me, still smiling. What annoyed me more, though, was the lack of surprise on her face. What, did masked dudes regularly interrupt coven orgies? Man, the supernatural world was fucking weird. No matter, she obviously thought I was going to be an easy mark.

Pity for her, she was wrong on a lot of levels and it was time for school to be in session. She slashed at me with her claws, a sloppy haymaker. I'd had the barest of combat training, a week spent getting my ass kicked in a krav maga class before realizing I had better things to do, but even I saw it coming a mile away.

I stepped into it and planted an armored fist into her face, pulling my punch a bit so that she definitely felt it, but it didn't come across as being delivered with superhuman strength.

Nevertheless, it had the desired effect. Her lip split, blood flew, and she stumbled back a step, dazed.

So this was what it was like to be winning a... "Oof!"

Something slammed into my back and I went down face first. There wasn't a lot behind the blow, but I'd been caught by surprise. What the hell?

I quickly rolled over, only to find Firebird's date standing over me holding a chair.

He raised the makeshift weapon. "Think you're tough, asshole?"

You've gotta be fucking kidding me. Did this shit-for-brains not realize his life was in danger? Actually, he probably didn't. I'd interrupted them before Firebird could show her hand. I'd need to refine my approach going forward.

First, though, I'd need to live through this.

Thankfully, my salvation came in the form of my intended foe. Firebird stepped in and caught the chair before the guy could bring it down on my head.

"This one's mine, lover." she said, flashing her fangs at him.

"What the fuck?" he gasped.

"Oh don't worry." She wrenched the chair out of his hands with little effort. "I love a man who's willing to stand up for a woman. I'll make sure you die with a smile on your face."

With that, she backhanded him and sent him flying over the couch.

Awesome! Well, maybe not for him. With the exception of Sally, I had a fairly low opinion of the folks under my charge. I considered them heavy on looks, but light in the brains department. I was happy to see that I wasn't going to be disappointed in my assumptions for a change. In one fell swoop, she'd laid her cards on the table and given me the opening I needed. Now to only hope she hadn't killed the guy with that hit. That would kind of defeat the purpose.

Oh well, I'd worry about him later.

Firebird grabbed me by my coat and dragged me to my feet, erasing any leverage advantage she might have had. I *thanked* her by driving my head forward and smashing the front of my helmet into her face. In the ongoing battle of carbon fiber versus noses, carbon fiber wins.

It wasn't a huge blow, but it backed her up a step.

She put a hand to her nose and eyed the freely dripping blood that rubbed off on it with a look of pure murder. "You're gonna pay for—"

I gently interrupted her tirade with a baseball bat to the kisser. "Your change, miss." I know I was supposed to keep my mouth shut, but goddamn it was just too much fun to throw out quips... especially when I was winning.

I socked her again with the bat and she went down to one knee. I'd seen how tough vampires were, and knew how quickly they could get back into a fight. The time for chivalry was over. I wound up and this time put everything I had into my swing, bringing the bat down against the back of her head with a solid *clonk*.

Firebird went down like a sack of bricks and lay there unmoving.

I looked her over, carefully in case it was a ruse, but she wasn't exactly a navy seal. As expected, she was out cold and looked like she'd been run through a trash compactor. Despite everything, a part of me felt bad, but then I remembered that the worst of it would probably already be healing by the time she woke up. Now to only hope she sought out the others before the last of the bruises faded, so as to tell them about her maniacal assailant.

Oh who the fuck was I kidding? Considering how fast word of my pussing out against Dusk Reaper had spread, I sincerely doubted I'd have to wait long before hearing about this.

The job done, I dragged the would-be hamburger helper back to his feet. He appeared dazed but otherwise unhurt.

After a few moments, his eyes cleared and they opened wide in panic. "What the fuck was that? What the fuck are you?"

"I'm a friend," I replied, loudly so Horndog could understand me.

"And her... that? What was...?"

I held up a hand. This was no time for exposition, not unless I wanted to give Firebird the baby seal treatment again. "All you need to know is that there are things out there beyond your understanding."

"My understanding?"

"To put it bluntly," I replied, not wanting to say the V word in front of this douche-nozzle.

"The hell with this shit, asshole. I'm calling the cops." Rather than run, like I hoped, he reached into his jacket for his phone.

Fuck that noise. I grabbed it out of his hands and crushed it, hopefully sending the message home. Remembering a line from *Blade*, I quickly added, "They own the police. They're everywhere."

"But what...?"

"Go home and forget about this. Pretend it never happened so you don't draw attention to yourself." I walked to the door and held it open for him. "And next time... bring more than just a condom for protection."

11

A CALL FROM THE CHIEF

"Like clockwork," I muttered as my phone began to chime.

I'd taken off my vigilante outfit in the stairwell before leaving the building, but this time I replaced my trench coat with a regular jacket. My hope was that my normal appearance cut a far different silhouette than my alter ego, just in case any other Village vamps happened to be lurking close by.

I was several blocks away, pretty much just randomly wandering and hoping to look like any other doofus out on the street this night, when my phone rang. Though I'd originally planned on heading straight home to debrief / brag to my room-mates, I decided to give it a little while. If Sally called while I was on the subway, that might give her cause to start dialing my home number. I didn't want to risk Tom answering and giving some nitwit excuse that could blow the whole thing.

"Hello," I said innocently into the receiver.

"Guess what just happened?" Sally asked from the other end. Her tone wasn't quite the panicky pitch I'd been hoping for, but then I remembered who it was I was talking to.

"You decided to start offering two for one specials on lap dances?"

"No, balls for brains. Someone just beat the shit out of Firebird."

"Oh?" I feigned a modicum of concern. "Is she okay?"

"She was well enough to whine about it." I couldn't help but notice the distinct lack of caring in her voice. Hell, if anything, she sounded amused. Guess Firebird wasn't at the top of Sally's Facebook friend list.

"What happened?"

"Hard to say for certain. She was at the 20th Street apartment when she says something kicked the door down."

"Some*thing*?" I asked, bemused that reality was already giving way to bullshit.

"Yeah. Whatever it was, it barged in and mercilessly beat the crap out of her. She claims she was lucky to escape with her life."

"Another vampire? HBC maybe?"

"According to her, it was like nothing she'd ever seen before. She keeps yammering on about something dressed in all black, like a demon out of Hell."

"Do you believe her?"

"She's a fucking idiot, what do you think? Personally, I think she got sloppy on a hunt, picked a not-so-easy target, and now she's trying to get some sympathy rather than just admitting one got away."

"Oh?"

"But that still isn't stopping her from telling anyone who'll listen." I was about to say something noncommittal, but she continued, "But you know what? Maybe this is a good thing for us. Lord knows I've been looking over my shoulder all week. Hopefully this will give them all something else to think about for a while."

I smiled into the receiver. Hopefully indeed.

"Oh hey, Bill?"

"Yeah?"

"Speaking of the HBC, did you happen to start some shit with those assholes again? I got a call from Colin earlier and he…"

"Sorry, the subway car is entering a tunnel. You're breaking up. Talk to you soon." I sputtered some static noises and quickly hung up. Colin, James's assistant, was the acting vampire in charge of Boston – the hub of undead activity in the Northeast. I'd only met him once, but he'd made a bad impression. The guy was a shit salad with extra asshole dressing. Worse, he seemed to have some history with Sally, a history that apparently gave him cause to enjoy fucking her over … and me by association. With James out of country, I had little doubt his overly-ambitious underling would take great pleasure in fanning the flames of unrest between the two prominent New York City covens.

"So did he at least thank you for saving his ass?"

"He didn't seem all that grateful," I groused, having brought my roommates up to speed on the night's events.

"Fuck it. The guy was an asshole with a case of the blue balls," Tom said. "What did you expect?"

"Probably true."

"That's okay, though. This was just your test run. Next time, you need to target one of the dudes in the coven. You save some sweet piece of ass from a big bad vampire and it'll be all the hero pussy you can get."

Ed let out a pained sigh. "Doesn't that kind of defeat the purpose of Bill being an *anonymous* vigilante?"

"Hell no. It makes it even better," Tom explained. "Remember that scene in Spider-man where he hangs upside down and lets Mary Jane roll up his mask so she can ram her tongue through the back of his skull? Well, do something like that ... except with your dick."

I got up and walked to the fridge to help myself to one of the blood packs stored there. Tom's moronic fantasies aside, as far as I was concerned it was Miller time except with a bit more clotting. "I think it's safe to say that your plan of me becoming a vigilante is probably the only good one we're getting out of you this year."

"Hey, if you want to spend eternity protecting

your virtue, go right ahead. Me? I'd take every grateful blowjob that came my way."

"Of that I have no doubt."

"Me neither," Ed added. "Probably the more stubble on them, the better he'd like it."

"Tom does have a point, though." Before Ed could open his mouth, I quickly added, "Not about the blowjobs. Firebird was an easy mark. I need to crack a few tougher nuts if I'm gonna make any real headway on this. I mean, Sally pretty much laughed her story off as a feeding gone bad. We need some more credibility if we're really going to scare these motherfuckers."

"You could target her," Tom suggested.

"Don't forget she knows where we live."

"Ed's right," I said. "Sally's a smart cookie. We make the wrong move around her and she's gonna figure this shit out in an instant and be kicking down our door."

Ed nodded. "As much as I wouldn't mind seeing her again, I'd prefer it be under less murder-inducing circumstances."

"Agreed. So she's out. That leaves the guys. Dusk Reaper is an obvious one. I wouldn't mind knocking that dickface down a few pegs, but maybe we'll save him for later. Brian is tough, but not too bright. Keith is a troublemaker, but he's a typical bully. He'd probably run crying home to mama the second he was outclassed. Those are our top choices. The rest, well, a few of them are real killers. Hell, I'm not sure I could win even if I had to put the bite on them."

"Maybe yes, maybe no," Ed replied.

"I'm pretty sure someone like Dread Stalker would hand me my ass."

Ed raised his hands in a shrug and smiled.

"Okay, and you're smirking why?"

"Because I know something you don't," and then to Tom, "and lots of stuff you don't."

"Such as?"

"Such as," he repeated, rising, "I kind of figured we might run into an issue like this. After Tom called me at my old man's and clued me in, I got to thinking. More importantly, I pulled Pop aside and got his thoughts on it."

"You didn't…"

"Relax. He'd think I'd gone soft in the head if I started spouting off about vampires and shit. No, I just wanted to discuss self-defense with him… see what he had to say about it."

"And?"

"And that's pretty much his favorite fucking subject in this world." He walked into his room, continuing to talk as he did. "So in the end I wound up borrowing a bit more than a spare can of deer spray. Figured I'd save this just in case we needed it."

I glanced at Tom and smiled. "He got me a shotgun too!"

"Are you fucking stupid?" Ed called from inside his room. "Seriously? What are you gonna do with one? Try shooting something like that off in the middle of fucking Manhattan. Subtle it is not. You use that in the Village and you're gonna get a lot more attention than just a few vamps."

He had a point there. I could trust that vampires

wouldn't go running to the cops. The people I saved were iffy, but the circumstances around their rescue were bound to be weird enough that most would be afraid of being laughed out of the precinct. Still, if I started blasting a boomstick in the middle of our territory, it was bound to attract unwanted attention. There was also a chance I'd slip and actually blow someone's head off. Truth be told, there was at best a small handful of Village Coveners I'd miss, but this whole exercise wasn't about killing them – it was about convincing them to not kill me. That would be difficult to pull off without any witnesses left behind.

No. This was a mission to sow fear, not leave a trail of bodies in my wake. There was also the small problem that I'd never used a firearm before in my life. For all I knew, I'd be just as likely to shoot myself.

Thankfully, Ed proved all of that speculation to be moot when he stepped out of his room.

"Ta da!" he declared in a faux cheery voice. "This, my friends, is the latest in military surplus stun guns. Guaranteed to knock an elephant on its ass or..."

I finished for him, a big grin etched across my face, "Or flash fry some vampire balls."

12

AWESOME ACTION MONTAGE

"I'm not saying you're full of shit. I'm just saying I don't really see any reason to panic over this."

"Did you see what that monster did to Keith?" Starlight asked, her eyes wide with fear. "He was almost killed."

That was a bit of an overstatement. I knew because, interestingly enough, I *had* seen what happened to Keith. I'd also seen what happened to Victoria and Brian before that. Hell, I'd gotten an up-close and personal look at my handiwork.

I'd also seen the damage they'd inflicted upon me one by one. Even armed as I was, fighting vampires was still risky business. I was no doctor, but I counted a couple of cracked ribs, several deep gouges in my side, and a dislocated shoulder among the injuries dealt me. The only difference between us was I'd limped home to heal up, making sure nobody saw my injuries. These whiners seemingly couldn't wait to find a shoulder to cry on.

Boo fucking hoo.

Despite all of that, I had to admit that shit had gone far more smoothly than I had any reason to expect. Four attacks thwarted over the course of the week, four humans saved, and four vampires sent packing with their asses handed to them. Even better, nothing had leaked out to the press... outside of a fifth page tabloid story that Ed happened upon after an extensive web search and, well, I didn't exactly see anyone other than conspiracy nuts paying attention to that shit.

It was all almost enough to make me cackle out loud. However, that might have come across as either suspicious, crazy, or both. So, instead, I settled for reiterating my lack of concern. "I can't believe I'm hearing this. Are you all seriously this afraid of some nutjob in a mask?"

The Loft was surprisingly full that night. Usually the only time there were this many vamps in one room was when Sally threw a party... typically neglecting to tell me about it in advance. They couldn't really all be that scared to be out on the streets, could they?

Firebird answered my silent question. She'd been otherwise occupied working through a fifth of tequila when she looked up. "I'm telling you, that isn't just some guy in a mask. I don't know what it is, but it isn't human."

"Oh? So then what is it?" I asked with a straight face.

"I don't know."

"I've heard rumors of wizards in the city," Dread

Stalker said, glancing around as if daring someone to ridicule him. "Maybe they conjured up something." If even he was spooked, then this was a pure gravy boat of awesome-sauce.

"Wizards? Did we step into a D&D game when I wasn't looking?" Unsurprisingly, my question drew blank stares from the crowd. Goddamn, these guys were starved for pop culture.

"What if it's an Icon?" All heads turned toward Starlight, silence descending upon the room.

Heh. James had mentioned those to me shortly before leaving on whatever business he had. They were some sort of magical warriors, imbued with the power of faith – the same anti-vampire magic that Tom had somehow infused his toy with some months back. Fortunately, they were just as rare, maybe even more so, than Freewills.

Regardless of how absurd it was, though, Starlight had unwittingly given me the perfect setup.

"No fucking way," Dusk Reaper muttered. "Just… no fucking way. If that's the case, then we're all dead meat."

Make that doubly perfect. Now was the time for my coup de grâce.

"Fine. Maybe it is an Icon, who knows? Stranger shit has happened." I stood and raised my voice. "If it is, though, I'll find it and kill it. And if it isn't, I'll still find it and kill it. It's time for this to end."

All eyes were now on me. There was no doubt in my mind that, long before the sun rose, every single vamp in the coven would have heard about their leader's awesome bravery. That ought to shut the fuckers up for a while.

"I'll hunt this thing down, whatever it is. When I do, I'm going to take revenge upon its ass tenfold." Time to have a little fun… not that I wasn't already enjoying myself. "As for the rest of you, you call yourselves vampires? You'd better hope when I'm finished with this thing that I don't decide to come back and take out the rest of my frustration on your cowardly—"

The door opened and Sally walked in, interrupting my badass monologue in one fell swoop, courtesy of the green mini dress she wore. It hugged her body so tight you'd have sworn it was a second layer of skin. The words caught in my throat as my eyes drank in the sight. Talk about a walking distraction.

"My apologies for the interruption, coven master" she said, her tone convincingly repentant despite that being complete bullshit. She was still aiming to keep our asses from being impeached with extreme prejudice.

I gave her an annoyed glare, only half acting. Bitch had ruined a perfectly good tirade on my part. "Your apology is noted. I was just telling our brothers and sisters that the hunter was about to become the hunted. Whatever is stalking Village Coven, be it man, beast, or Icon."—I threw in that last one just to make them flinch—"is about to learn what happens when you cross the Freewill."

To my immense satisfaction, a wave of relief passed visibly through the crowd. Their doubt in me

RICK GUALTIERI

appeared to be gone, and in its place I saw the worshipful reverence that I liked to believe I deserved. It was good to be the king.

Unfortunately, Sally had to go and ruin the moment by opening her fucking pie hole. "With all due respect, I believe that's a mistake."

"What?" I did my best to mouth "shut the fuck up!" to her as subtly as possible, but she either didn't understand or was purposely ignoring me.

"We can't risk you. The Boston prefecture has decreed that you're too important. There are other warriors in the coven. We can send them instead to…"

"I knew it," Dusk Reaper said.

"Excuse me?" she asked.

"This is all a ruse."

"I don't know what you're…"

"Liar!" he spat. "Do you think us stupid enough to fall for these lies?"

What?! Oh fuck! Don't tell me the shit-for-brains actually figured out what I was trying to do.

"Hear me, brothers and sisters," he said, turning to face the others. "Our so-called master is weak."

Oh crap.

"He never intended to hunt down our enemy. His bravery is only a false front meant to deceive us. Can't you see that this was his plan all along? I say he conspired with Sally Sunset to…"

"What did you call me?" Sally asked, her eyes narrowing.

"The name our true master, Night Razor, bestowed upon you."

Shit had just gotten real. Of all the stupid code names that had been handed out to Village Coven by the old regime, hers had potentially been the worst. She'd kept her first name, but had made it clear that the Sunset part was to be dropped lest she drop whoever dared utter it.

"Why you little—"

But Dusk Reaper wasn't quite done yet. He stepped back, pointing an accusing finger at her. "Confess! You and the Freewill devised this ruse. Did you think we wouldn't notice your convenient timing - stepping in and stopping him from hunting an enemy he never intended to face? I say all of this was so you could save his pathetic life at the expense of sacrificing more of ours."

That's what he thought I was doing? Guess he really was as dumb as he looked.

Or maybe not. Judging by the angry glares reappearing throughout the crowd, he'd definitely struck a chord.

"Oh?" Sally asked, her voice flat with anger. "Is that so?"

"Do you deny it?"

"I do. I say the Freewill is no coward. He wouldn't hide behind such a sad little conspiracy."

"Actions speak louder than words, bitch."

Oh boy. This was getting ugly fast. Why the fuck did she have to come over when she did? I had been just about to seal the deal.

"I think I see what this is really about," she said. "You think you'd make a better master than Bill, don't you?"

Dusk Reaper smiled in return. "I do, for I would lead us in Night Razor's name and continue his ways." He turned to the others and raised his voice again. "The killing, the blood, the fun! Who remembers that?"

All of the guys in the room nodded, most of the ladies too. In fact, only Sally, me, and—interestingly enough—Starlight seemed to not find that idea too peachy keen.

"Very well," Sally replied, her tone betraying no sense of urgency. "Then as you yourself said, actions speak louder than words."

Oh no. The crazy bitch was gonna suggest a trial by combat between us. Dusk Reaper might have been a pussy at heart, but he was still a great deal more experienced than me. I opened my mouth to say something, but she picked that moment to continue.

"Village Coven is under siege and it needs to end now. What I propose is simple enough. You and the Freewill will compete to see who finds and ends this threat first. The winner will be acknowledged as the one true master of this coven."

13

___

A BREAK BEFORE THE BLOOD SPILLS

Silence reigned in the room for several seconds. I glanced at Dusk Reaper and saw a glimmer of doubt in his eye, but he noticed me staring and quickly covered it.

"So be it," he said. "We will find this—"

"There is no *we*," Sally interrupted. "This will be a contest between the two of you."

Oh, I could tell Dusk Reaper didn't like that one bit, but he was in too deep to back down now. "Very well, but how do I know this isn't another trick?"

To my surprise, Sally crossed the room to where he stood. I found myself hoping she was gonna give him the mother of all cock punches, but instead she stood upon her tiptoes and leaned in to his ear. She whispered something, too low for even my hearing to pick up.

When she stepped back, he was smiling. "Rejoice, for soon we shall once again own the night!"

Goddamn, the formal speech he used when trying

to sound important really irked me... almost as much as Douche Reaper himself. I didn't know what Sally told him, but I had to trust it was good... maybe a free blowjob or something. That sure as shit would've convinced me.

Regardless, this was workable. I could still salvage Tom's plan and end this in my favor.

But first I would need to teach Dusk Reaper a lesson.

Okay, first, I needed to have a little word with Sally. It was getting late... or early; I still didn't have my brain wrapped around vamp hours. Either way, not much would be happening this night. I mean, Dusk Reaper could start his hunt whenever the fuck he wanted to. Hell, if I so chose, he could stand out on a street corner for the next week trying to ambush our so-called stalker. The truth was, nothing was going to happen until I put my costume on and made an appearance. The only way Dusk Reaper could try winning otherwise was if he decided to start killing random dudes dressed in black and then pass them off as me—which, knowing the idiot, he might. Ugh, I so despised being master over such a group of vacuous dipshits.

The coven appeared mollified by our competition, which was apparently as good as I was destined to get. After I short while, I slipped away, managing to catch up with Sally as she walked back toward the Office.

I casually sauntered up to her. "Nice night."

"Yep."

"Heading back to the Office?"

"Still plenty of work to be done there," she replied in a matter of fact tone.

"So… what did you say to Reaper?"

"And why is it any of your business?"

"As coven master, I could order you to divulge."

"You could. And as your partner, I could tell you to take a flying fuck off the nearest building."

"True enough," I replied, continuing our leisurely pace through the city streets. "But, I'm gonna ask anyway."

"It's simple," she said, turning to face me. "I told him what he wanted to hear. I stroked his ego a bit, dangled the carrot of coven leadership in front of his face. Think about it. It's a tantalizing prize for a self-absorbed asshole like him. This way he also doesn't have to face you in fair combat."

I considered what that could entail. Vampires had a pretty fucked up concept of fair. "He'd probably win."

"Yes, but he doesn't know that. He has just enough doubt to be a fly in the ointment, but not quite enough to man up and grow a set on his own."

"But he agreed to this hunt."

She turned with a grin and continued walking. "Of course. Nobody said this hunt had to be even remotely fair, did they?"

Using that logic, it would be best for me to watch the skies for the inevitable nuclear strike.

We walked for a few more minutes in relative

silence then, just for argument's sake, I decided to test the waters a bit. "But what if he wins?"

"That would suck."

"It would..."

"For him."

"Huh? How?"

"Do you honestly think the rest of this group is going to tolerate that asshole being in charge for long? I'd give him a month tops before he ends up dust in the wind. Hell, I might even do it myself if it came down to that, but it won't."

"It won't?"

"Nope, because you're going to win."

"How do you know?"

"I was standing at the door listening for a few moments. I heard you. You weren't afraid."

Uh oh. I needed to play this coy. Unlike the rest, Sally was sharp—sharper than any blade I'd ever seen. "Maybe I'm too stupid to be."

"I leave that as a distinct possibility, but I prefer to think that maybe you're starting to get the hint of how things work. I think maybe, just maybe, you're beginning to believe in yourself as a vampire." She glanced my way and smiled, for once not displaying her normal shark-like attitude. "If that's the case, then I should too."

"Really?"

"I mean it."

I was touched. Holy shit. This was a side of Sally I hadn't seen before.

I'd been planning on spilling my guts to her about the vigilante as well as the plan my roommates and I had concocted, but now I hesitated. Who would it really hurt to play out this ruse? Well, Dusk Reaper for sure, but fuck him.

The thing was, Sally actually had a little faith in me—even when I didn't. I hadn't a clue why. Hell, I wasn't even sure it was possible. Nevertheless, a part of me didn't want to let her down. Everything I was doing was bullshit, an act meant to save my own ass, but maybe her belief in me could inspire me to become more. Maybe in time I could be the person she believed me to be… assuming that person wasn't a cold-blooded murderer of course.

I moved closer and made to put my arm around her shoulder, but a quick sidelong glare told me we weren't quite at that level yet. Oh well. I'd work on that one.

For now, hopefully it was enough for me to say, "I won't let you down."

14

THE THRILL OF THE HUNT

I decided to let Dusk Reaper stew for the night. Hopefully he'd found some dank alley to stand around and look impotent in. Me, I hopped on the subway and headed for home. I'd left my outfit there and, also, I needed to fill my two personal sidekicks in on the plan change.

Once home, well, I decided to get some sleep first. I'm not a fucking moron. An all-day planning session on how to best set up Dork Reaper was best tackled if I wasn't dead tired. I tell ya, even with my vampire physiology I still had no idea how superheroes did it. You'd think at some point Nick Fury would just crash the fucking helicarrier into the side of a mountain because he fell asleep at the wheel.

Anyway, late morning found us sitting in our living room with me giving them the lowdown on the night ahead.

"This could work out even better than we originally

planned," Tom admitted. "If you lay this asshat out and then manage to *defeat*"—he held up his fingers in air quotes—"the stalker yourself, well, I'm pretty sure that's the last peep you're ever gonna hear out of him."

"I doubt it, but at least he probably won't be able to cause me any more trouble. His credibility will be shot to shit."

"Okay, so let's do this."

I held up a hand. "Not so fast. Sally was good enough to warn me that it was pretty much anything goes as far as this hunt was concerned. It's possible Reaper could be armed... hell, knowing this limp-dick, it's more than likely. I can handle a knife or a lead pipe, but if he's packing heat then that could be trouble."

"Agreed," Ed said. "Sounds like we need to scout him out in advance."

I considered his words. I wasn't keen on involving them, being that they were both human and thus a lot squishier than me. Conversely, they'd proven their mettle against Jeff. Also, if I said no, the fuckers would probably just follow me anyway. At least this way I could keep an eye on them.

"Fine. I won't lie. I could use both your help on this one. This isn't just about running interference with Dusk Reaper. This is the end game. Tonight, I finally destroy the scourge of the vampire race once and for all. It needs to look good."

"I'm in," Ed said with no hesitation.

"Fuck yeah," Tom added.

"Awesome. You guys are my Bucky and Speedy."

Ed raised an eyebrow. "Um, let's not use those names."

"You're right," I replied. "They're already taken anyway. I know. You're my Faggy and Douchey. I'll leave it up to you to decide who's who."

Tom was quick to fire off, "Dibs on Douchey."

Ed was equally quick to raise both his middle fingers. The pact thus sealed, we raised our beer cans to the victory that was ours for the taking.

The downside of having humans for roommates was their obvious disadvantage in a fight against creatures who could punch holes through cinderblock. The upside, though, was that they were nothing but cattle to most vampires. That made them beneath contempt and thus practically invisible. It also didn't hurt that the only other still-living (sorta) member of the coven who'd met them was Sally and she wasn't a part of this. As a result, I had what amounted to the equivalent of ninjas on my side, minus maybe any fighting ability.

The first part of our plan had been to ascertain where Dusk Reaper was hunting that night. I mean, it was a big city and even with vampire senses I could have gone days without crossing his path and that was just within our territory.

Rather than overthink this, I simply stopped by the Loft. As expected, it wasn't empty, although it wasn't nearly as full as the night before. Guess the rest of the coven had decided to hole up elsewhere while

Reaper and I conducted our manhunt. Of course, it was also possible that Sally had put their asses to work over at the Office and the folks here were just the lucky ones who'd escaped.

Either way, a few curious eyeballs turned my way. It was far better than angry glares.

Finally, Eliza asked me, "Aren't you going out hunting? Dusk Reaper is gonna find this guy first if you don't."

Interestingly enough, her tone wasn't dripping with fondness at the mention of his name. Sally had once mentioned to me that a good hate fuck could be a wild thing every so often. Maybe that was the case here. Or maybe the asshole just couldn't get it up. Yeah, I definitely preferred that scenario.

"Afraid he'll win?" I asked casually.

She looked uncomfortable for a moment, as if she didn't want to say anything, but then apparently thought better of it. "Kinda. I mean he's fun to hang with, but I don't really want to go back to the way it was."

I was going to question that, but then I remembered the sensation of Night Razor's fist ramming into my face with the force of a jackhammer. It was something I was certain most of them had felt at some point or another. "Don't worry. Neither do I."

It was good to see not everyone wanted to go back to a system where there was one master and everyone else was basically a slave. Sure, I might be a nice enough guy that I'd slipped into the dreaded friend zone with the women here, but hopefully at least a few appreciated that I didn't treat them all like my personal fuck toys.

Anyway, the hook baited, I decided to see if I could reel in my catch. "I'd better get going and find a good spot. Wouldn't want Reaper trying to swoop in at the last minute and steal my kill."

"You might want to avoid the area down near West 10th then. I think that's where he said he was staking out."

And BINGO was her name-o. "I'll do that, thanks."

"Good luck, Bill."

I smiled back at her. Now to see if I couldn't nudge luck ever so slightly in my favor.

"Really, the warehouse?" Ed asked from the driver's seat of his hatchback.

"Yep, real original isn't he?" I replied, changing into my black combat duds in the tight squeeze of the back seat.

It was all I could do to not roll my eyes when I learned where Dusk Reaper was hunting. The coven had a safe house down there, an old warehouse. I knew it well. It was where Night Razor and I had finally faced off.

The place looked abandoned, but that was by design. The reality was it served as a spot where the coven could congregate in times of emergency, complete with sewer entrance and state of the art surveillance system. It was actually a smart pick by him. If he got into trouble, it gave him a place to retreat where he'd have the advantage.

Of course, that assumed his attacker wasn't aware of its true nature. Sadly for him, I both knew the place and also had the security codes to get in. Sally didn't share much of what she knew about Village Coven, especially the bank records, but she made sure I had enough knowledge to not get locked out in an emergency.

"Everyone ready?" I asked as Ed pulled to the side of the road a few blocks east of our target—just another car double-parked in NYC.

"Fuck yeah," Tom cried with a fist pump. He was definitely enjoying this a bit too much. It almost made me glad it was ending tonight.

The plan was simple enough: once we took down Dusk Reaper, it would be time for me to vanquish the Village Coven stalker once and for all. That part was simplicity itself, mainly because it was already done. Since it had always been a part of the plan, we'd taken the liberty of taping it a few days prior.

Ed had been wearing my stalker getup, complete with some extra padding. Tom had done a fairly good job of acting like a random pedestrian who'd stumbled across an epic battle and filmed it with his phone from a safe distance, oohing and aahing all the while like he was scared shitless. We'd gone back and forth – Ed the silent warrior, me snarling like some kind of fucking jungle cat. It had been *close*, but in the end the script called for me to be the triumphant victor.

The plan was for the video to "leak" onto YouTube sometime later tonight. In the meantime, we had a cooler of bagged blood in the trunk to smear all over the smashed biker helmet that would sadly be all that remained of the poor stalker once I was finished with him. Combined, I'd have proof of my victory. Even if there were naysayers, they'd be silenced once it became obvious the attacks had stopped.

It was fucking genius.

All we had to do was get past one dipshit who looked like a reject from a Winger concert. Once he was out of the way, we'd be home free.

Hosed down with extra deer scent, just to be safe, I scouted the area from the shadows – taking my time closing in on the location. I might not have enough experience to pick out a vampire by scent alone, but at least he wouldn't have that advantage either.

Tom and Ed hung back for now, one on foot and the other circling the area with his car.

There! I spotted the douchebag smoking a cigarette about half a block away from the warehouse. It wasn't hard to pick him out. This area didn't get a lot of pedestrian traffic after dark, at least not of the up-and-up variety.

It occurred to me that this was an odd spot for him to hunt. Even a total retard should've been able to figure out that the vigilante's MO was to strike when a vampire had a victim in their sights.

Of course, that might have been part of Reaper's plan. I'd gotten a taste of his personality and at heart the guy was a fucking coward—a bully when the odds were in his favor, but quick to turn pussy once there was a shred of doubt. Perhaps he was betting on returning to the coven and claiming that the stalker was too scared to go after him when all along it was him looking to avoid a fight.

Well, too bad for him. I had other ideas.

I slunk back around the side of the building I'd been using as cover and dialed Tom's cell. "He's two blocks west of you. Be careful."

"He's the one who'd better be careful, because I'm gonna—"

"Just shut up and do what you're supposed to." He was like a brother to me, but goddamn sometimes I wanted to punch his lights out.

Tom had volunteered to be a combination of wingman and bait. His job was to get close enough to Dusk Reaper to ascertain if he was packing any serious heat. That was my main concern. A couple of forty-five slugs to my body could really ruin the evening. It wasn't perfect. I mean it's not like Tom could perform a full body cavity search on the asshole without getting killed, but a casual bump on the street might at least clue him in.

That's the point where things could get dicey. All I could hope was that we'd planned for every contingency.

I glanced again around the side of the building, saw my friend come into view, and quickly donned my helmet.

It was show time.

15

HOT PURSUIT

Tom's cover was simplicity itself. He sported a half bottle of Jack and was acting like he was pissed to the gills.

I saw Dusk Reaper turn in my roommate's direction. He tensed for a moment, but then relaxed when he saw it was just some drunken dipshit. So far, so good. I glanced further down the block, scanning for headlights. Even with my night vision it was hard to tell one car from the next, but I didn't worry too much about Ed. He knew the plan and was reliable. Chances were he was in position and waiting for his signal.

Should Tom ascertain that Reaper was armed to the teeth and, assuming he was allowed to go on his way, he'd signal me with a loud drunken rendition of *Hit Me Baby One More Time*. That would be my cue to text Ed to drive down the block and run the asshole of a vampire over.

What? I never said I planned on being sporting

about this. Besides, that was just our emergency equalizer.

A part of me was definitely hoping we'd need to use it, though. After all, seeing that twat-waffle get mowed down would be intensely satisfying. At the same time, I needed to remember it was a worst case scenario.

Tom reached where Dusk Reaper leaned against the side of a building, smoking like he was in an eighties Motley Crue video. Still acting the drunken fool, something Tom had a lot of experience with, he wandered over and tried starting up a conversation, all of it easily audible to my ears.

"Spare a smoke, man?"

"Fuck off," Reaper growled. A real people person that guy.

"Come on, bro." Tom staggered forward right into Reaper. He practically fell into the vamp's arms, giving him a good chance for an impromptu frisking.

I held my breath. The problem with vampires was that, much like a rabid animal, they could be unpredictable. A psycho like Night Razor might have just snapped a person's neck right out in the open, not caring who saw it. I was betting, though, that Reaper didn't have quite that set of balls on him.

"Get the fuck off me, motherfucker!" Reaper gave a shove and my roommate went stumbling back, the bottle falling out of his hands and shattering on the sidewalk. I tensed up, ready to race over, regardless of whether it might be into a hail of gunfire.

Fortunately, the vamp hadn't put everything he had into the push. Tom lifted himself off the ground, apparently unhurt. Thank goodness. Despite their insane enthusiasm to help me, I still hated getting them involved in the affairs of the supernatural world. Shit could turn sour in an instant and, even with my speed, I doubted I'd be fast enough to always stop it.

Tonight, though, the stars appeared to be smiling down upon me.

"That all you got, tough guy?" Tom slurred. "You're just a dickless loser!"

That was it—his signal that he hadn't noticed anything on Reaper. It wasn't the most eloquent of call signs, but then again Tom had come up with it.

Our version of "whiskey, tango, foxtrot" given, I slipped the bat out of my trench coat and gripped it tight in my right hand.

Sadly, Tom's code phrase also had the downside of being just a tad infuriating to people who actually were dickless losers. Before I could spring into action, Reaper had crossed over to my roommate and grabbed him by the jacket.

"When I'm done with you, we'll see who has no dick," he spat, baring his fangs.

Shit!

"Maybe," Tom replied, all trace of drunken slur gone, "but at least mine won't be on fire."

With that, he pulled Ed's stun gun from his pocket and made himself a fried asshole sandwich.

The weapon had been at my insistence. Though I hated to lose the advantage it afforded me, there was no way I was letting my friend walk into danger without at least something to help even the odds.

Despite my hope that he wouldn't need to use it, I found myself smiling nevertheless as I took off at full speed toward the two, especially since Tom was giving him a good long jolt.

Unfortunately, vampires are a hardy bunch. Reaper went down twitching, but he still managed to have enough sense to get a foot up and kick out at Tom – catching him in the chest. My roommate went flying, landing in the middle of the street.

Judging from the chorus of curses that erupted from his mouth, he was just stunned. Now to only hope Ed didn't accidentally run over his stupid ass. As for me, I raced past my roommate, doing my best to not convey any sort of familiarity just in case things went south.

Reaper was already up on one knee by the time I reached him. That was mighty obliging as it put him at the perfect height. His eyes opened wide with surprise just a second before I connected with a left-handed uppercut.

Unlike my first outing with Firebird, where I tried to hold back a bit so as to give no clues to my preternatural strength, I put everything I had into it. My armored fist connected with his jaw and there came the distinct sound of teeth shattering – oh so satisfying a noise when it wasn't my own.

Dusk Reaper went rolling ass over teakettle back the way he'd came, spitting blood as he went.

Sadly for me, his age gave him a bit of extra resiliency over the others I'd *introduced* myself to.

However, it hadn't done much for his courage. He managed to roll back to his feet before I could use his noggin for batting practice and turned tail—no threats of revenge or not seeing the last of him, he just spun around and ran.

In hindsight, I should have accepted my victory and been happy with it. Instead, I took off after him. He was, after all, the primary source of my irritation as of late. Between being a steadfast supporter of the old guard, trying his best to turn the rest of the coven against me, and actually getting some ass whereas my dating life lately consisted of Pornhub... well, he was the living embodiment of all the shit I thought I'd left behind when I'd taken over.

The dumb fuck didn't even try to be subtle as he ran, accelerating quickly to a speed no human could hope to match. Oh well, it's not like the streets were packed. Our only witness was Tom and it wasn't like he was gonna tell anyone. I followed suit, matching his pace. I wanted to put a hurt on him. Then, when I showed up at the loft later, complete with the battered remnants of my stalker outfit, there would be no doubt left in his mind that I wasn't someone to fuck with, even if it was all smoke and mirrors.

Screw it. I wasn't proud.

It didn't take a genius to figure out where Reaper was headed—the warehouse. He was probably hoping to double back and catch me by surprise in the warren of crates that filled the building like some sort of rat maze. Worst case, he could always try to slip down the sewer entrance and make an escape. Pity for him that I wasn't nearly as ignorant of the layout as he was no doubt hoping.

He raced around the side and my ears picked up the distinct sound of the main door being shoved open. Fine, I could play this game.

But that didn't mean I cared to play it stupidly. I slowed down and reminded myself that Dusk Reaper was a vampire. Pussy though he was, if cornered he could still be deadly. I needed to be coy about this, give him a false sense of hope.

Making my way to the warehouse entrance, I hesitated for a few moments, waiting until a human pursuer might reasonably have made it here.

That done, I used my bat to push open the door just in case his big plan was to hope I was stupid enough to stroll in and be ambushed. No sign of him, so I entered.

The lights were off. That didn't mean shit for a vampire, but I didn't care to show my cards quite yet. I crept forward, my hands reaching out in front of me, pretending that I was feeling my way along blindly.

All the while, I was scanning every nook and cranny for movement while keeping my ears peeled for any sound that might give him away. I debated how I wanted to play this. It might make sense to let him think he got the drop on me, give him a false feeling of superiority before bringing down the hurt.

I was considering making some noise, maybe pretending to stumble, when the choice was made for me.

My damned cell phone began to ring.

16

HERO'S WELCOME

Goddamn it! I fumbled my phone out of my pocket, and quickly hit the answer button, all the while cursing my stupidity for not putting it on vibrate.

"What?" I hissed

"Did you get him yet?" Tom asked.

"No, I didn—oof!"

Something hit me from behind. What a surprise.

I flew headlong into a large wooden crate, smashing through the side. Thankfully, the blow had hurt my pride far more than my body. I quickly rolled over, ready to defend myself again, but there was nobody there.

Was that his tactic, hit and run?

If so, he was gonna be sadly disappointed. I'd deserved that one, but from here on out I'd be a lot more careful.

"Yo, you still there?"

I raised the receiver to the side of my helmet.

"Remind me to kick your ass later."

"What for. Did you—"

I ended the call and powered down my phone, silently vowing revenge upon my idiot roommate. Getting back to my feet, I dusted myself off and again tried to home in on any sounds, all while trying to look as lost as Little Red Riding Hood in the deep dark forest.

There! A noise to my left.

I reached an intersection among the crates and made to turn that way, only to hear another sound, like feet shuffling, off to my right.

I wasn't sure if Reaper was using his speed to try to confuse me, or if maybe it was just the acoustics of the place.

Either way, it definitely creeped me out a bit. Scenes from nearly every horror movie I'd ever watched came racing up from my subconscious. It was not helping the situation. Fuck me. Now was not the time for this shit. My opponent was powerful, but not nearly at the level Jeff had been. He was also running scared. I needed to remind myself that I was the boogeyman of this movie. I was the Jason Voorhees here, not him.

More noises filtered through my helmet, seemingly coming from multiple places at once. What the hell?

I remembered Sally's words that there was nothing to guarantee that this hunt need be a fair one. Had I underestimated Reaper? Had the stakes at play caused him to up his game? Was it possible that in trying to spring a trap I'd instead walked into one?

Those weren't the most pleasant of thoughts. A part of me debated retreating, but I realized I was nearly at the heart of the warehouse. The way back wasn't much shorter than the way forward and I didn't care to let Reaper think he had me on the run. No. He was far more likely to be unnerved if I kept coming.

Again, I had to remind myself that I was an unknown quantity to him. He had no clue who I was or what I could do. If I kept pushing, kept up the illusion of fearlessness, he would break first.

My eyes continually searching for movement to go along with the noises, I reached the clearing that I knew lay at the center of the building. It was the exact same spot where I'd squared off against Jeff.

Note to self: once this was over and done with, reorganize this fucking place.

I stepped out and made my way to the very center, leaving a good twenty feet of open space on either side of me. I stopped and listened, my instincts telling me that if something was going to happen it would be now.

The shuffling noises began again, first to the right, then to the left, and then behind me. I realized my mistake. I'd been focusing on sight and sound alone. Had I taken the time to use my nose too, I'd have surely concluded that there was more than one scent in the building—much more.

At that moment the lights of the facility flipped on, blinding me. It didn't matter. I didn't need to see to know that I was surrounded.

Still momentarily dazzled as my eyes adjusted to the bright interior lights, I was hit from the side. It was a glancing blow, but it staggered me nevertheless. I turned, raised a fist, and then stopped in my tracks as I saw Starlight advancing upon me. Hesitation and fear shone in her eyes, but the two by four in her hands was apparently giving her some extra courage.

What the fuck was she doing here?

Sadly, I could have asked that question more than once.

More vampires stepped out into the open space—Brian, Victor, Firebird and more: about a half dozen in total. Definitely not the full coven membership, but a lot more than I'd been expecting.

"Well, well, well, what the fuck do we have here?"

I spun to find Dusk Reaper finally making an appearance, the grin on his face so smug you'd have thought he'd just finished judging a dick sucking contest.

The vamps continued to advance, surrounding me, but not quite within my reach yet. I was still an unknown to them, or so I tried to convince myself so as to keep my knees from shaking.

"Thought you were smart, didn't you, freak?" Reaper asked. "Well, you weren't smart enough. Didn't even consider the trap I set, did you?"

"Eh hem!" a voice called out from somewhere further off in the building.

I glanced in the direction it came from. A catwalk ran the perimeter of the warehouse at about the second story level, high enough to give someone a pretty good view of the whole place. It wasn't empty.

My jaw nearly dropped when I saw Sally standing upon it, smug amusement on her face as she looked down at us.

"Suggested, of course," Reaper corrected, "by my new second in command."

I knew it! That fucker was neither smart nor popular enough to organize this little soiree. Sadly, my small satisfaction was greatly overshadowed by the blow of seeing that I'd been set up by the one vampire whom I'd been sure was on my side.

She smiled in my direction, a predatory grin if ever there was one. "Teach this freak a lesson," she said, then leaned back against the wall to watch the show.

"You don't give the orders here!" Reaper shouted at her.

Sally turned her attention to him, her expression souring. "Perhaps, but you're not in charge yet."

Unfortunately it was that *yet* part that was the kicker for me. What a fucking cunt!

"Then I shall make sure to remedy that," Reaper replied disdainfully.

Sadly, before I could voice my opinion on things, he pointed a finger and the vamps converged on me.

I didn't see any way to avoid a major ass-beating, but that didn't mean I was going down easy. Hell, I could always start crying for mercy *after* they'd pummeled me into paste. As far as backup plans went, that would have to do.

For now, I spun in an arc, swinging my bat in an attempt to keep them at bay. It worked about as well as I expected.

Starlight and Firebird jumped back, but Brian wasn't nearly that bright. I connected with the side of his head as he rushed forward. It was a solid hit that sent him to his knees, but it killed any momentum I had with the weapon. Before I knew it, a set of hands had ripped it out of my grasp.

A second later it was returned—at full force into my gut. I doubled over, the wind knocked out of me.

More hands, these sporting claws, grabbed hold from behind and dragged me to my feet, gouging deep furrows into my shoulders in the process.

I was spun around, and caught a fist to the jaw. My helmet absorbed the brunt of the impact, but it was still hard enough for me to see stars. Thankfully, years of being harassed by jocks in high school had taught me a few survival skills. I instinctively ducked, certain another punch was incoming from somewhere. I was right. This one was from a vampire who went by the stupid moniker of Shadow Fury. He went high and I managed to get below it. I straightened my body and sent him flying over my shoulder.

Go me!

Unfortunately, that seemed destined to be my swan song in this fight as I spun just in time to see Firebird step in. Before I could raise a defense, she raised a knee… to my crotch. I knew I should've added an industrial strength athletic cup to my outfit.

Sadly, I hadn't, and thus got to experience the wonderful sensation of my nuts being smashed so far into my body that I'm surprised I didn't cough them out.

That took the fight right out of me and I went down to my knees.

"Let's kill this fucker," a voice from behind me growled. I might've cared were I not ever so slightly preoccupied with my poor crushed balls.

"Not yet," Reaper said from somewhere in front of me. I couldn't help but notice that of all the vamps who'd just tried to get a piece of me, he hadn't done shit to dirty his pretty little fingers. Pussy.

"Hold him," Reaper commanded. For a second nothing happened. Heh, what a loser. "Do it!"

That finally got them moving. I was dragged back to my feet and my hands yanked rudely away from cradling my two best friends.

I shook my head to clear the cobwebs and looked around. Starlight was holding onto my right arm while Victor had my left in an iron grip.

Now that I was restrained, Reaper strode up to me. The sporting guy that he was, he took a moment to drive a fist into my gut ... hard enough to make me momentarily forget my family jewels. "I want to look into our angel of death's eyes while we teach him what true terror is."

He grabbed hold of my helmet and yanked it off.

"Not angel," I said, spitting up some blood. "Doctor."

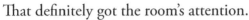

That definitely got the room's attention.

"Bill?" Starlight asked, loosening her grip on me.

"You!" Reaper spat, quickly covering up the look of surprise on his face.

That started the crowd a muttering. Disbelief and shock seemed to be tonight's blue plate special. I glanced up, expecting to see a similar look upon Sally's face. At the very least, that might have given me some satisfaction before these fuckers dusted my ass. However, her gaze remained passive, her green eyes staring into mine as if I'd just announced nothing more interesting than the weather.

I swear if I get out of this...

Oh wait, I probably wasn't going to. At least that seemed to be Dusk Reaper's plan. He picked up a discarded two by four and snapped it over his knee, leaving one piece with a nice pointy end. "We end this now."

"Yep." My voice was barely a squeak, but I knew he heard me. "Because that's the only way you're gonna win this."

"Silence, betrayer!"

"Betrayer?" I asked, thinking quickly. Maybe there was still a way out of this. "I don't answer to you or anyone else here."

"And that gives you the right to terrorize... err... attack your own?" he replied, quickly backpedaling on the T word.

"I am master of this coven. My word is law and if I decide the rest of you fuckers need a lesson in humility, then you're going to get it in whatever fashion I so decide."

"You *were* master of this…"

"I still am," I spat, my voice stronger as I tried to project an aura of authority, "unless the rest of you prefer to follow a vampire who doesn't have the guts to become master by his own hand."

That definitely caught their notice. There was only one crime in a vampire coven, so far as I knew, and that was appearing weak. Reaper wasn't the oldest in this group. There was no way he'd be able to hold onto power for long if he started his reign off on a questionable note and he knew it.

"I don't need to prove anything to you."

"No, but you need to prove it to them."

I glanced around and was amazed to find most of the vamps in the room taking a step back. Holy crap, they'd swallowed my bullshit. A moment later, Victor released his grip upon me and did the same. Starlight alone remained where she stood, the expression on her face one of a deer in the headlights.

I smiled. "So, I guess the question is, are you challenging me to fair combat?"

Reaper's fangs descended. He knew he had to put up or shut up. "I am."

"You got it, asshole."

With that, I reached out and grabbed hold of Starlight. Dragging her in, I bared my own fangs and sank them into her neck before she could stop me.

Vampires had a very liberal interpretation of fair, after all, and it was about time I used that to my advantage.

17

FAIR COMBAT

Starlight screamed as I tore into her. Honestly, I kinda felt bad about it. She was one of the few vampires whom I actually gave a shit about. Unfortunately, she had three things going for her that were perfect for me at that moment. She was close by, she was older than me but not so much as to fuck me up before I could bite her, and if I were willing to attack her then it would surely send a signal to the rest that they'd be fair game no matter what.

At first it was close. She almost shrugged me off, but then that first mouthful of blood hit my stomach and my body instantly reacted to it, adding her power to my own. I held on for a few more seconds, more for the effect than anything else. I took a few greedy slurps and maybe copped a feel too—hey, I never claimed to be applying for sainthood—then pushed her to the side with a grin.

She hit the floor and lay there sobbing. It made

me feel like a real shit, but I needed to keep my resolve, otherwise this whole thing would fall apart.

Thankfully, my actions had the desired effect. The jaws of every vamp around me practically hit the floor in shock. They'd all heard the stories, but this was the first time any of them, save Sally, had seen it in action—vampire myth made reality—and they were terrified. I wasn't about to let the opportunity pass me by.

"I tried to be nice," I said slowly, my fangs out and on full display. "I wanted us to have a new beginning, forget the past. I even kept my distance and my hands to myself. I didn't ask for much, just that we try to curb our base nature, to stop acting like fucking animals!" Oh, how I wished someone was taping this. "You'd think I wasn't asking for much, but no. You had to flaunt my rules." I turned to glare directly at Dusk Reaper. "You had to challenge me. So I decided that a lesson was in order; that you all needed to learn what it was to fear the dark again."

Steeling my gaze, I glanced at each of them, partially for intimidation purposes, but also to gauge whether I was about to be dogpiled en masse.

Focusing again on Reaper, I continued, "I'd hoped that would be enough, but I see now that more is required. I am the legendary Freewill of the vampire race. Face me if you dare."

Oh snap! Judging by the look on his face he'd just dropped a load in his pants. Maybe some days this gig wasn't so bad after all. Of course, I was potentially writing a check that my body couldn't cash, but these fuckers didn't need to know about that.

Dusk Reaper was backed into a corner and he knew it. He needed to either shit or get off the pot. Facing me was uncertainty itself. He had no way of knowing that at best my power was on par with his. For all he knew, my next act would be to drag his ass out onto the street and beat him to death with a Mack truck. Backing down meant his credibility in the coven was shot—he'd no longer be able to say shit against me—but it also meant life. I wasn't Night Razor. I knew the concept of mercy.

For a moment I could see the choice waging war inside of him. Then he averted his eyes and looked down.

Holy crap was that it? I'd won without throwing a punch? Hot damn! That's the beauty of cowards, they always chose to live to fight another day.

I let out a breath and relaxed my posture, the tension draining out of me.

Yeah, I should have realized my mistake in thinking I had a chance in Hell of ever being that lucky.

Reaper looked down, as if just now remembering the makeshift stake in his hand, and charged me.

Guess he decided to shit after all. I just hoped it wouldn't end up being on top of my grave.

Dusk Reaper closed the distance between us with frightening speed, a reminder that he was three times my age. I'd let my guard down for only a second, but it was more time than he needed.

Weapon pointed at my heart, he rammed it home with a solid *clunk*.

The collision knocked the breath out of me, but I was certain that was nothing compared to the agony of dying that was sure to follow.

Wait... *clunk*?

A second passed and I couldn't help but notice I wasn't busy turning to dust.

That stupid baking pan under my shirt! It might never again be undented enough to reheat pizza, but it had saved my ass nevertheless. Holy shit. I'd thought it by far the stupidest part of Tom's plan, yet it had turned out to be pure brilliance.

Reaper, for his part, seemed stunned that I was still standing there. His eyes opened wide in surprise and his gaze met mine—just in time for me to drive a fist into the side of his face with a wild haymaker. The strength of two vampires, augmented by brass knuckles, proved a formidable combination. Blood and teeth flew, as Reaper dropped the splintered remains of his stake and spun from the impact.

Not one to look a gift asshole in the mouth, I threw another punch to the back of his head, hoping I scrambled his brains real good.

I knew I wasn't much of a fighter, but I really didn't need to be. All I needed to do was press my advantage, throwing blow after blow into his stupid fucking face. Oddly enough, my conscience offered few moral qualms against doing so.

It didn't take long before Dusk Reaper, his face bruised and bloody, went down to his knees.

I grabbed him by his long hair to hold him up as I raised my fist and readied to knock his block off.

"All hail the Freewill," he sputtered weakly.

I paused mid-swing. "Excuse me?"

"All hail the Freewill," he repeated in a slurred voice. "All hail the rightful master of Village Coven."

That's exactly what I wanted to hear and, more importantly, what the rest of the vamps in the room *needed* to hear. With that, the fight was over. I'd once more solidified my position as leader of this pack of bloodthirsty monsters.

"Thank you. Oh, and by the way, my name is Bill." And *then* I punched his lights out.

Fair combat, indeed.

Any other coven master would have dusted a challenger's ass without a second thought, but that wasn't my style. I'd killed a vampire in self-defense, and hopefully wouldn't hesitate to do so again. But straight out murder? No, I wasn't there yet. With any luck I never would be.

Instead, I faced the rest of the crowd and asked if there were any other challengers. Unsurprisingly, there weren't.

I can't say for certain I saw actual respect in their eyes, but gone was the open rebellion—for now. I'd take it.

I ordered them to pick up Reaper and get the fuck out of there before I changed my mind about them all. I was relieved to see no hesitation on their part. None met my gaze upon leaving, save Starlight. I felt really bad because what I saw in her eyes was fear. I'd need to make it up to her, but it would have to be at another time. For now, I needed them to do what I knew they all would—spread the word to the others before the hour was out.

Maybe that high school mentality wasn't so bad after all.

After they filed out, I called up my roommates to give them the all clear.

Tom began peppering me with stupid questions, which I of course started to embellish in my answering, but then I spotted movement out of the corner of my eye.

Sally stepped out from the maze of crates and into the opening opposite me.

A flash of hot anger hit me at the sight of her. I said, "I'll fill you in when I get home," and hung up without another word.

"That was well done," she said, without even a hint of remorse.

"Well done? You have a lot of nerve saying that after fucking me over."

"Pretty sure I didn't do anything that had to do with you and fucking."

"I'm not in the mood for jokes, Sally. You lied to me."

"Yep."

"All that stuff you said you told Reaper…"

"Guilty as charged." She held her hands up in mock surrender. "Why do you think he accepted the challenge so readily? I told him we'd set a trap and he'd be sure to walk away as coven master."

"So this was a set up?"

"From the start."

I gritted my teeth. How the hell could she be so smug about what she'd done? "So all that bullshit about having faith in me. That's exactly what it was, bullshit."

To that, she appeared surprised. "No. I meant it. I knew you'd come out on top. It would be hard not to against a loser like Reaper."

"Cut the crap. You set it up so that he'd trap the vigilante. If things hadn't worked out like they had, the rest of the coven would be tearing me limb from limb right now."

To my surprise Sally rolled her eyes. "Do I really look that stupid?"

"What?"

"I asked a question. Do you really think I'm that stupid; that I didn't figure out you were the one in that stupid costume the second I heard about it?"

That caught me for a loop and for a second I was silent, but then I remembered what a master manipulator she was. "Bullshit. You had no way of…"

"Oh please." She leaned against a crate and folded her arms across her ample chest. "A mysterious vigilante showed up in our city and started specifically targeting vampires, leaping out of the shadows to save their victims then disappearing just as quickly."

"Yeah and?"

"*And* it's straight out of a fucking comic book. If that had really happened, you'd have creamed your pants so hard there'd be a snail trail all the way back to Brooklyn. Hell, your fucking nerd herd roommates would have joined you in the circle jerk. But instead you acted like you couldn't have cared less." She puffed out her chest and lowered her voice. "You were all like 'I fear not this enemy of my people.' There was so much horseshit there, I'm surprised I didn't drown in it."

I stood there blinking like an idiot as I absorbed this. "Really?"

"Really."

"But all of this…"

"All of this is *exactly* what you needed. I've been filling their heads with Freewill crap, but that only goes so far. They needed to see it with their own eyes. And now that they have, I doubt you'll have to worry about any of them for a while."

"How did you know it would work out?"

"As I said, I had faith in you. Don't ask me why, but I had a feeling that if push came to shove, you'd come through."

"And if I hadn't?"

At that, Sally unzipped her purse. She reached inside and pulled out the biggest handgun I'd ever seen.

"If you hadn't then you would have still won. I'd just have needed to do a little extra recruiting for the coven when it was all over."

I stared hard at her, my mouth agape, trying to sense if there was any deception in what she was telling me. In the end, though, I had to accept a simple truth: I'd underestimated her once again. I'd thought I was the puppet master, when all along she'd been pulling my strings.

She walked up and slipped an arm around mine. "Come on, coven master. I could use a drink. It's been a long night."

That was the truth. "Okay. Maybe we'll make it a double."

"But first you need to lose the stupid costume."

"This?" I replied in mock horror. "How dare you profane a hero's uniform? Besides, doesn't it turn you on just the slightest?"

"Nope."

"You could be the Black Canary to my Green Arrow."

"Don't push your luck."

"The Lois Lane to my Superman?"

Sally patted her purse. "Care to see if you're bulletproof?"

"Maybe some other time." I laughed as we walked out of the warehouse. Knowing the life I'd found myself thrust into, I had a feeling there was a pretty good chance of that happening sooner rather than later anyway. For tonight, though, it was enough to know I could hang up my cape and enjoy the rest of the evening in peace.

THE END

Bill Ryder will return in
Scary Dead Things (The Tome of Bill – 2)

One of the most powerful vampires on the planet wants Bill's head. A crazed immortal princess wants the rest of him. It's a toss-up which fate is worse.

Bill's only hope for survival is to marshal his friends, master his powers, and somehow prove that, in a world of supernatural terrors, he's the scariest dead thing of them all.

Available now from Amazon.com

BONUS CHAPTER
SCARY DEAD THINGS

The Tome of Bill - Part 2

Note to self: don't listen to Ed's advice. Traffic was surprisingly light for a Sunday night. I was sitting in the passenger seat of Ed's two-seater piece-of-shit, watching the miles slide by. My roommate was behind the wheel. We were heading south on Route 287 toward the Outerbridge Crossing. He had been good enough to come down and give me a ride back home, which kind of made sense as it had been his counsel that had given me cause to want to flee back to the relative safety of Brooklyn. Nevertheless, I was glad for the ride. It had turned out to be a long weekend, and I was in no mood to deal with the idiocies of mass transit to get back home.

Since it was early Fall, there was no Jersey Shore traffic to contend with. Even so, considering it was only about six PM, traffic was pretty light heading toward Staten Island. It was that lull that tended to happen around late September or early October. People were still burnt out from the summer, and the holiday rush was a good month or so off. This was one of those rare times when people mostly stayed put. In short, the asshole ratio on the roads was low. I liked times like this. Sadly, they were too few and far between as of late.

We had been listening to some rock music on the radio, or at least what the DJ was calling rock. There were very few real rock stations left in Jersey. Most played either classic rock, which was mostly tolerable, or a combination of lousy ballads and pop rock (*which had barely enough guitar riffs to be outside of the Justin Bieber demographic*). We had been discussing how kick-ass rock music was such a rare commodity when my cell rang.

I'd been expecting it. I picked it up and answered with an innocuous, "Hello?"

"William, is there something you would like to tell me?" asked my Dad.

Uh oh. That wasn't a good sign. If he was calling me William, it meant he had noticed the little *mistake* I had left behind from my weekend of house sitting.

I decided to do what I did best, play dumb. "Nope. It was a quiet weekend, Dad."

"I'm sure it was," he replied in a tone that said he didn't even remotely believe me. "Your mother and I appreciate you coming down and keeping an eye on the place while we were at the beach." The *beach* in this case being the many casinos down in Atlantic City.

"No problem, Dad! Anyway, well I gotta..."

"Hold it!" commanded the voice on the other end. "I guess I won't beat around the bush. What the hell did you do to Angel?" At the mention of her favorite cat, I could hear my mother wailing and carrying on in the background. It pretty much sounded like she was in the middle of a major freak-out. Not too surprising, all things considered.

"Mom sounds kind of upset."

"I noticed," my father said, sarcasm oozing out of his voice. "Do you want to know why?" he asked, despite the fact that I had a pretty good idea and he most likely knew it.

"Why?" I asked innocently.

"Because right now she's vacuuming up a pile of Angel dust."

"Angel dust? You know, she should hold on to that. I hear the street value's off the charts if it's the good stuff."

"I'm not laughing, William."

"Sorry, sir," I automatically replied, despite being an adult, having a job, living on my own, and ... oh yeah ... being a freaking vampire. "What happened?" I asked, genuinely curious. After all, I wasn't *entirely* sure how things had played out ... especially since I'd made it a point to bug out before my parents got home, even going so far as donning a hoodie, sunglasses, and ski mask so as to brave the daylight without bursting into flames. It probably wasn't the manliest way I could have handled the situation, but I've always thought there's a fine line between bravery and idiocy. Sticking around would have definitely crossed that line.

"When we got home, your mother noticed the cat was acting a little strange," my father explained. "It was hissing and carrying on."

I again adopted an innocent tone. "They're cats. They go loopy every now and then."

"Don't be stupid. You know Angel," he chided. "You could step on the stupid cat's ... sorry, dear ... head, and she wouldn't bat a whisker. But not today. When we got home, she was going absolutely nuts. And there was something wrong with her eyes. They had gone all black like a shark's. That definitely was *not* normal."

"Distemper?" I unhelpfully offered.

"Not unless it was the most extreme case of distemper there's ever been," Dad continued. "Your mom was a mess. Made me go get the cat carrier so we could rush her to the vet." Oh boy, I think I knew where this was going. "I had the damnedest time getting her in it, too. Little bitch kept going after me."

"She didn't bite you, did she?" I hadn't considered that earlier. I wasn't even sure she could pass it back to humans, but it was a risk I wasn't really willing to take ... at least not with my parents.

"No, but she came damn close. I had to put on some work gloves to finally get her in. Then it got weird."

Yeah, I bet it did. "I'm listening."

"Your mom got in the car, but I had left my wallet in the house. I sat the cat carrier out on the walk and went back inside to grab it, and then..."

"In the sun?" I asked, already knowing the answer.

"What?"

"Did you leave the carrier in the sun?" I repeated.

"I don't know. I guess so. What does it matter?" he asked irritably. "All I know is that one minute it's quiet, and the next I hear your mother carrying on like a mad woman. I ran back outside, and do you know what I found? The cat carrier was on fire. I'm not just talking a few sparks either. It was like someone doused it with rocket fuel."

I was definitely starting to get a sinking feeling in my stomach.

Dad continued with his gruesome tale. "By the time I got the hose, though, the fire was already out. The damnedest thing was the cat. I was expecting her to be all burnt up, but there was nothing left. She was completely vaporized. All that was left was a pile of ashes with her collar sticking out of it."

"Wow. That's ... bizarre," I said, severely under-stating the whole thing.

"Yes, bizarre is one word for it. So that's why I want to know whether or not anything odd happened this weekend while you were around."

"No idea," I lied. "Like I said, Dad, it was a slow weekend. Barely saw the cat. She kept to herself. Other than that, not much going on ... hello, Dad? Dad? I'm losing you. We're heading into a tunnel. I'll buzz you back when..." and then I disconnected the call as I had no idea what else to say.

Ed and I drove on for another mile or so, and

then he said, "I know I only caught part of that conversation..."

"I don't want to talk about it."

He ignored me anyway. "But was that about what I think it was?"

I sighed and decided I might as well confess. It was going to be a long drive otherwise. "My mom's cat, Angel..."

"Yes?"

"I kinda, might have..."

"Yes?"

"Turned her into a vampire," I finished.

"YOU WHAT?!" he yelled, just barely managing to keep the car from swerving off the road.

"Turned it into a vampire."

"Why?"

"It was an accident."

"How was it an accident?"

"Well, as you had suggested, I got pretty wrecked this weekend," I said with a guilty grin.

"And how does that lead to an immortal demon cat?"

"Well, like I said, I was pretty messed up. I guess when vampires get the munchies they don't automatically go for the nachos like everyone else."

"That's fucked up, man."

"I know."

"It's your *mom's* cat!"

"*Was* my mom's cat."

"I mean, I don't even like cats," he continued, "and I still think that's fucked."

"Yes, I get it. I didn't mean to vampirize the damn cat. It just kind of happened."

"Is that even a word?"

"It is *now*," I snapped. "And then when she woke up from it..."

"I'm listening."

"I guess I kind of fooled myself into thinking that maybe I had dreamt it all."

"I take it from your dad's call that you were wrong on that front."

"Definitely not a dream."

"Fucked up," he repeated.

We drove on again in silence for a few minutes until I heard Ed chortle. I turned to see him grinning and trying ... and failing ... to suppress laughter.

"What's so funny?" I asked.

"I was just thinking..."

"Yeah?"

"There is a bright side."

"Do tell."

"When we get home, you at least get to tell Tom about how you got to eat some pussy this weekend," he said, finally cracking up laughing.

"Not funny," I said, but it was a lie. Put that way, it was actually pretty goddamned hilarious. I soon joined my roommate. We laughed for a good long while until my phone rang again.

"Oh shit," I said, tears still pouring down my face.

"Time to get back on the clock, my man," Ed commented.

He was right. I couldn't put this off. I just hoped I

could think of something to tell my parents that sounded more convincing than, "Sorry for vampirizing your cat, Mom and Dad." I picked up the phone and answered it.

"Listen. Tell Mom I'm sorry about her cat."

"Tell her your damn self," replied Sally from the other end. "I'm not your goddamned answering service."

"What?" I blurted out. "What are you doing on the line, Sally?"

"Oh, I don't know. I was lonely, what with you on *vacation* and all, and thought maybe I'd give you a buzz so you could talk dirty to me. But I'm afraid I have to draw the line at letting you call me mommy … or daddy, for that matter," she quipped.

"I can think of a few other words for you."

"I'm sure you can, but think of them while you're packing. Vacation's over."

"What?"

"You heard me," she said with an impatient sniff.

"Why am I packing?"

"Because that's what people do when they take a trip, unless they plan on traveling naked, and if that's your plan then please let me know so I can make sure I never have the same itinerary as you."

"Hold on. What trip?"

"The one you're taking," she said as if speaking to a moron.

"Why don't we start over, and you tell me what's going on?"

"I thought you'd never ask," she replied in that annoyingly chipper tone she adopted whenever she knew she was pissing me off. "You're going to China."

"What?! Why the hell would I be going to China?"

"James's orders. He called and requested your presence."

"Why?"

"Beats me. You can ask him that in person in about two days."

"I don't even have a passport," I protested.

"Wow, that's kind of sad," she said. "Not surprising, mind you, just sad. Fortunately, you don't need one."

"Why wouldn't I need a passport to get into China?" I asked. "Pretty sure they check those things there."

"Because it's a long flight, and since commercial airlines tend to have rules against their passengers going up in smoke when sunlight hits them, I made some alternate arrangements."

"Define *alternate arrangements.*"

"You, my friend," she replied, putting even more chipperness into her voice, "have been booked into a first class coffin in the cargo hold."

"WHAT?!" I screamed into the phone.

"You're welcome. By the way, you might want to pack a pillow." *Click.*

Bitch!

Scary Dead Things
Available in ebook, paperback, and audio

ABOUT THE AUTHOR

Rick Gualtieri lives alone in central New Jersey with only his wife, three kids, and countless pets to both keep him company and constantly plot against him. When he's not busy monkey-clicking words, he can typically be found jealously guarding his collection of vintage Transformers from all who would seek to defile them.

Defilers beware!

THE TOME OF BILL UNIVERSE

THE TOME OF BILL
Bill the Vampire
Scary Dead Things
The Mourning Woods
Holier Than Thou
Sunset Strip
Goddamned Freaky Monsters
Half A Prayer
The Wicked Dead
Shining Fury
The Last Coven

BILL OF THE DEAD

Made in United States
North Haven, CT
08 November 2022

26447523R00093